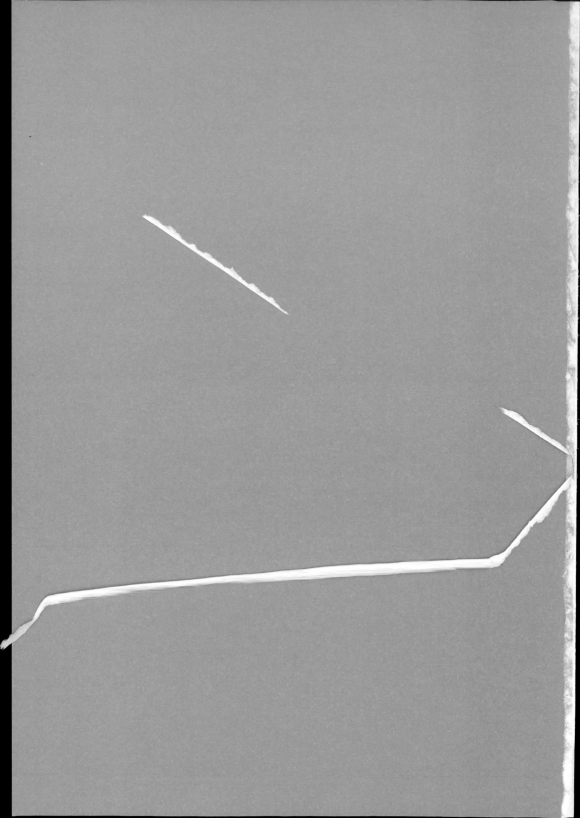

SECRET CODERS

Secrets & Sequences

GENE LUEN YANG & MIKE HOLMES

:01

First Second

New York

"It was this wonderful time between magic and so-called rationality."
–Wally Feurzeig, co-creator of the Logo programming language, on the early days of Logo

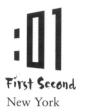

:01
First Second
New York

Published by First Second
First Second is an imprint of Roaring Brook Press,
a division of Holtzbrinck Publishing Holdings Limited Partnership
175 Fifth Avenue, New York, New York 10010

Library of Congress Control Number: 2016938729

Paperback ISBN: 978-1-62672-618-5
Hardcover ISBN: 978-1-62672-077-0

Our books may be purchased in bulk for promotional, educational, or business use. Please contact your local bookseller or the Macmillan Corporate and Premium Sales Department at (800) 221-7945 x5442 or by email at MacmillanSpecialMarkets@macmillan.com.

FIRST EDITION

First edition 2017

Book design by Rob Steen

Printed in China by Toppan Leefung Printing Ltd., Dongguan City, Guangdong Province

Paperback: 10 9 8 7 6 5 4 3 2 1
Hardcover: 10 9 8 7 6 5 4 3 2 1

BY ART WE LIVE

Chapter

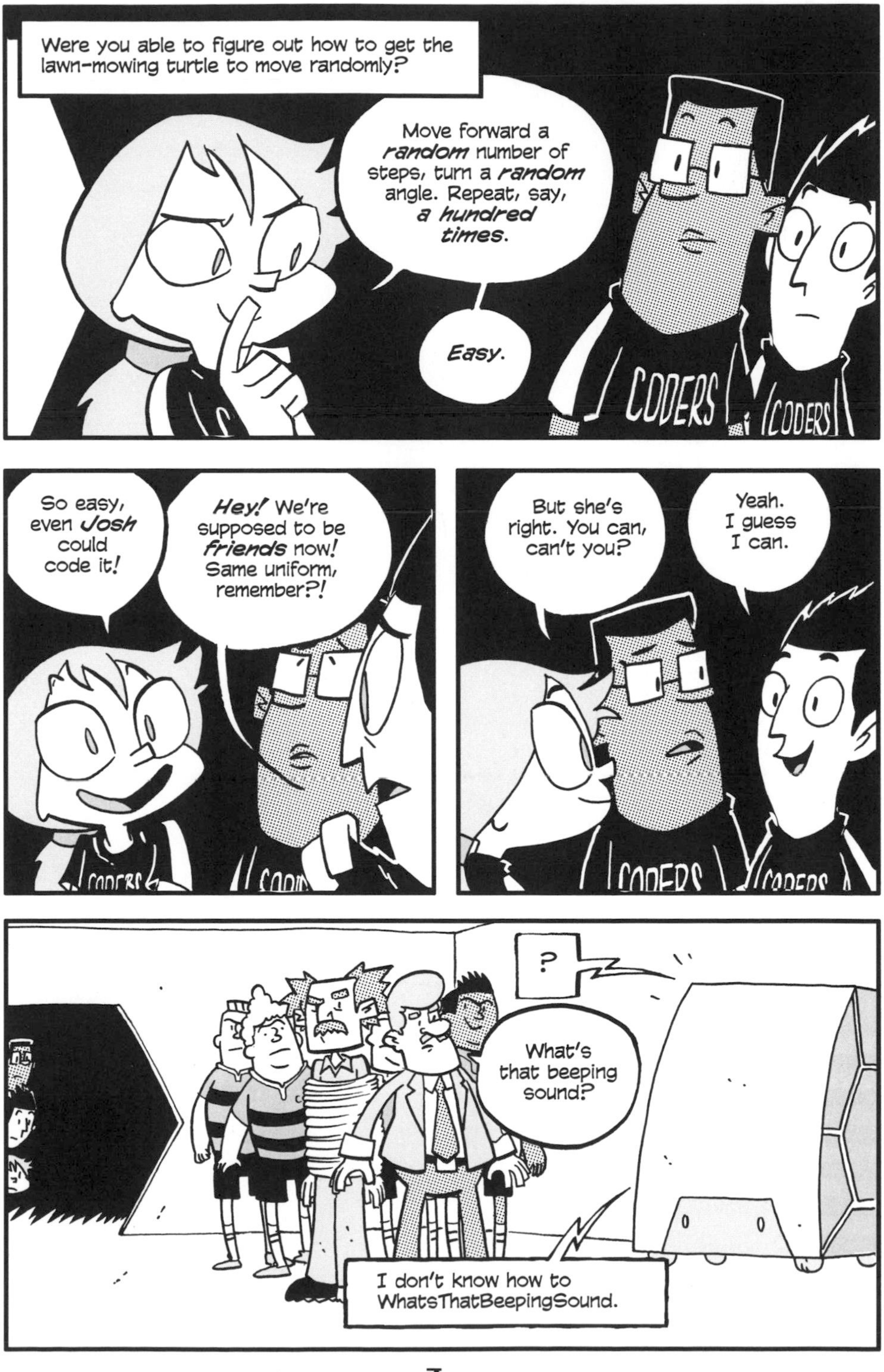
Were you able to figure out how to get the lawn-mowing turtle to move randomly?
Move forward a *random* number of steps, turn a *random* angle. Repeat, say, *a hundred times*.
Easy.
CODERS
CODERS
So easy, even *Josh* could code it!
Hey! We're supposed to be *friends* now! Same uniform, remember?!
But she's right. You can, can't you?
Yeah. I guess I can.
?
What's that beeping sound?
I don't know how to WhatsThatBeepingSound.

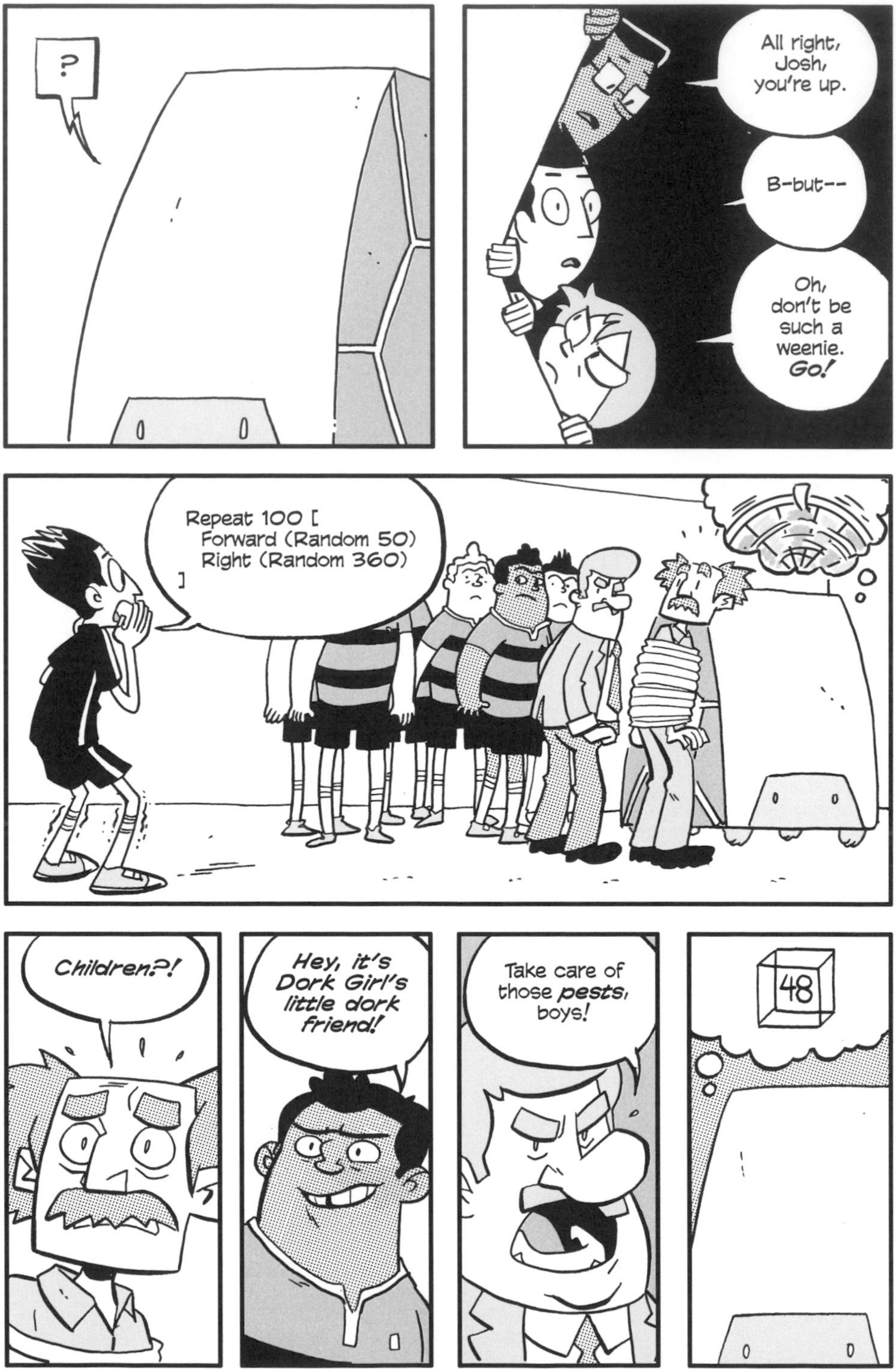
?
All right, Josh, you're up.
B-but--
Oh, don't be such a weenie. *Go!*
Repeat 100 [
Forward (Random 50)
Right (Random 360)
]
Children?!
Hey, it's Dork Girl's little dork friend!
Take care of those *pests*, boys!
48

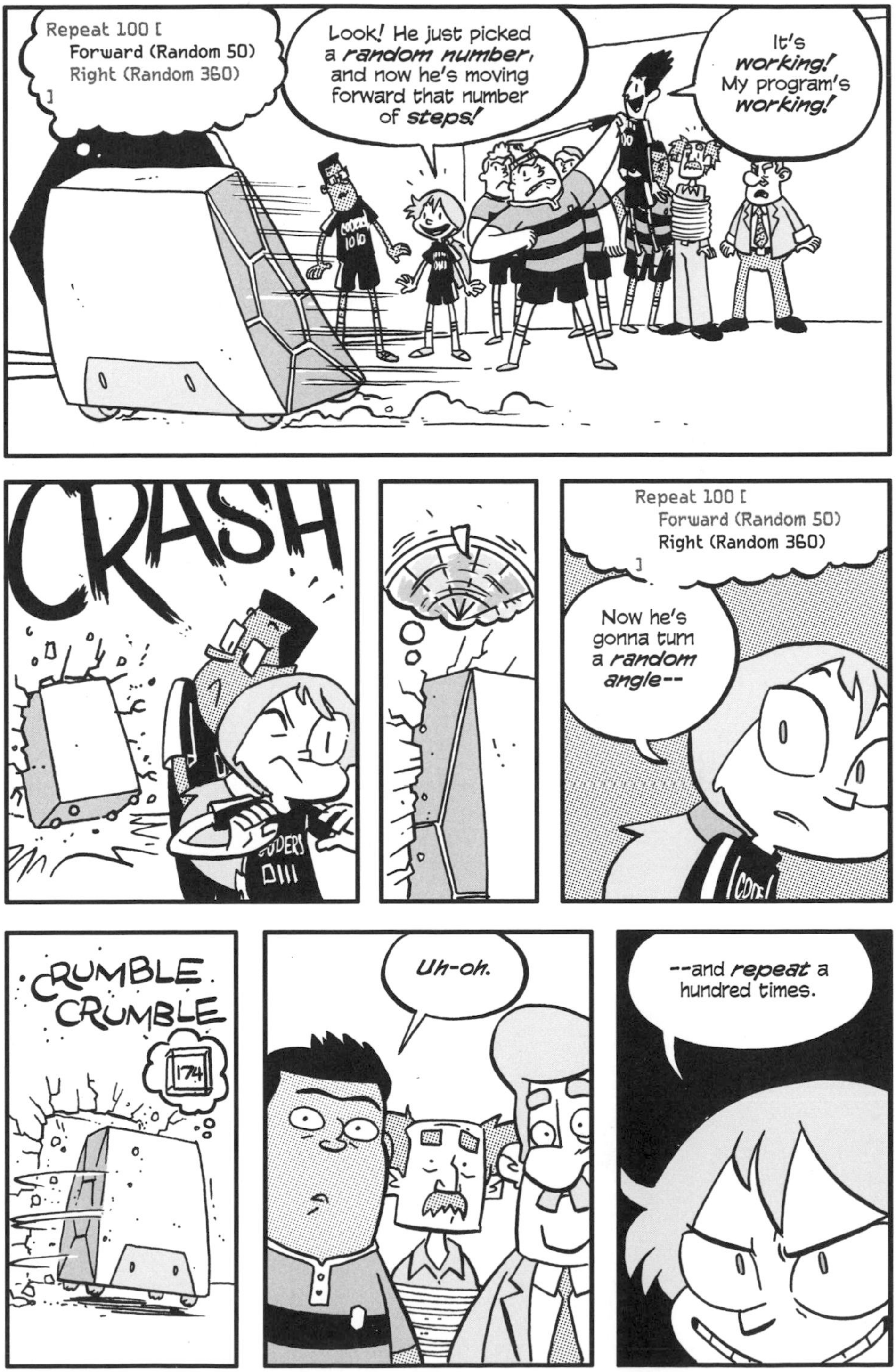
Repeat 100 [
Forward (Random 50)
Right (Random 360)
]
Look! He just picked a random number, and now he's moving forward that number of steps!
It's working! My program's working!
CODERS 1010
CRASH
CODERS
Repeat 100 [
Forward (Random 50)
Right (Random 360)
]
Now he's gonna turn a random angle--
CRUMBLE CRUMBLE
174
Uh-oh.
--and repeat a hundred times.

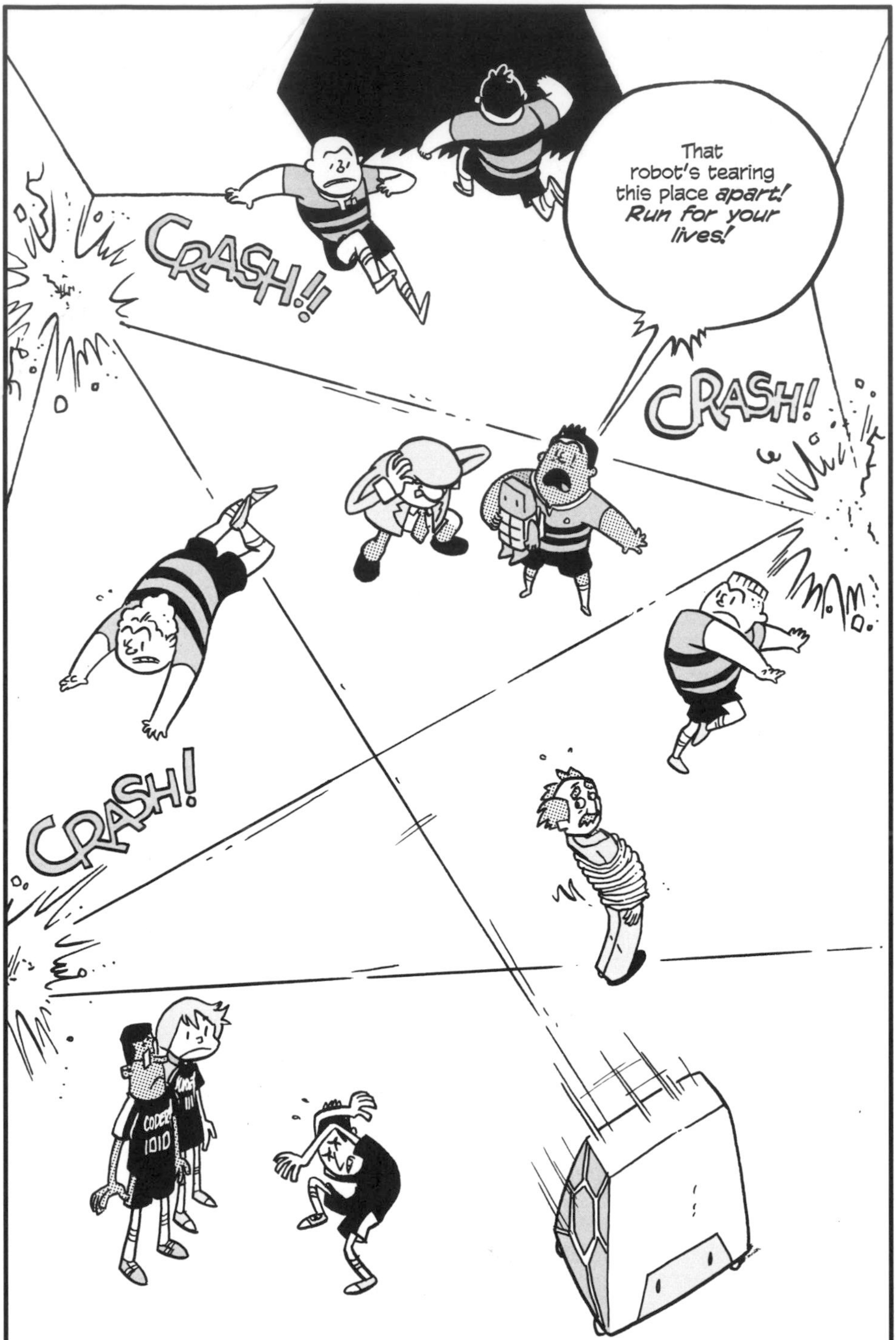
That robot's tearing this place *apart!* *Run for your lives!*
CRASH!!
CRASH!
CRASH!
CODER 1010

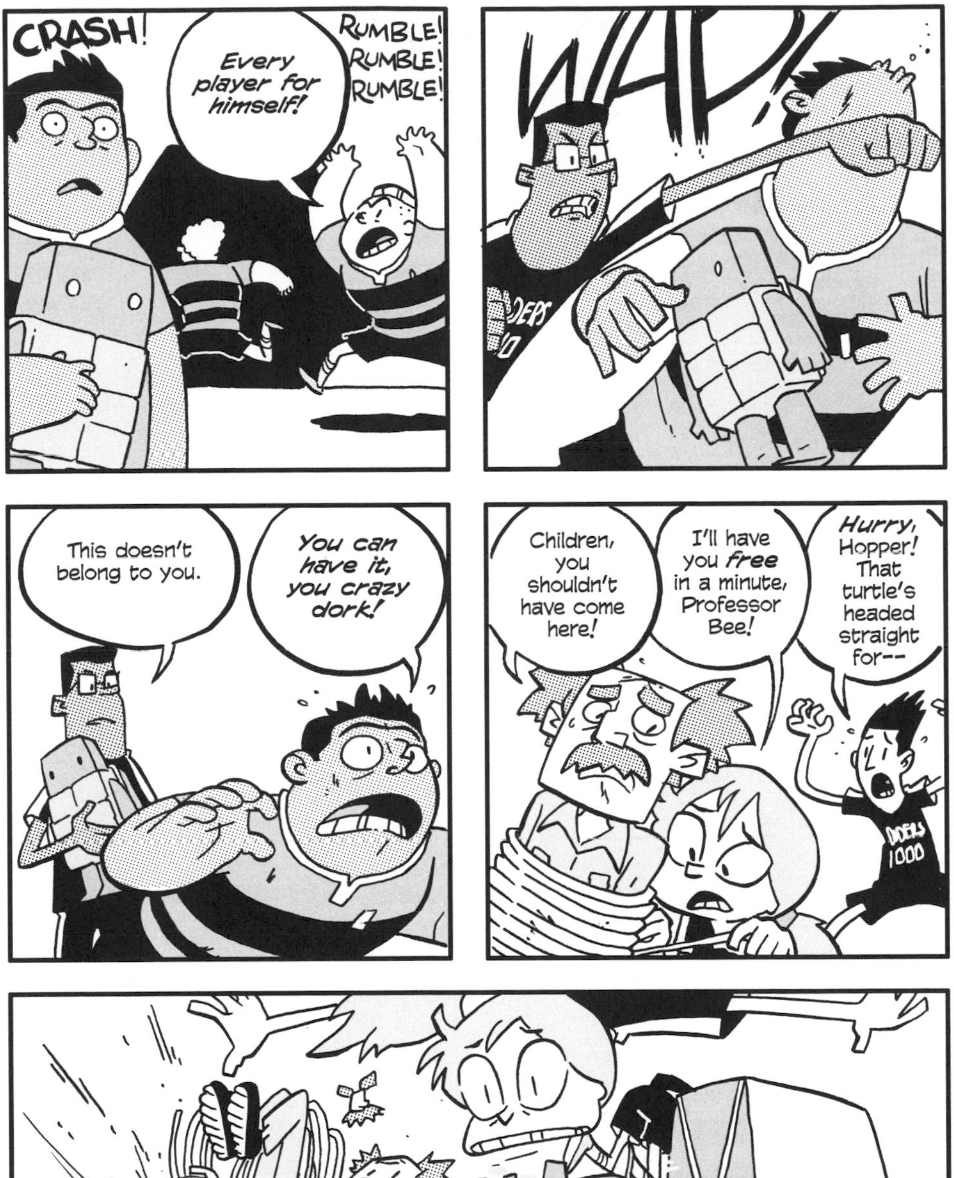
CRASH!
Every player for himself!
RUMBLE! RUMBLE! RUMBLE!
WAP!
This doesn't belong to you.
You can have it, you crazy dork!
Children, you shouldn't have come here!
I'll have you free in a minute, Professor Bee!
Hurry, Hopper! That turtle's headed straight for--
WHUMP!

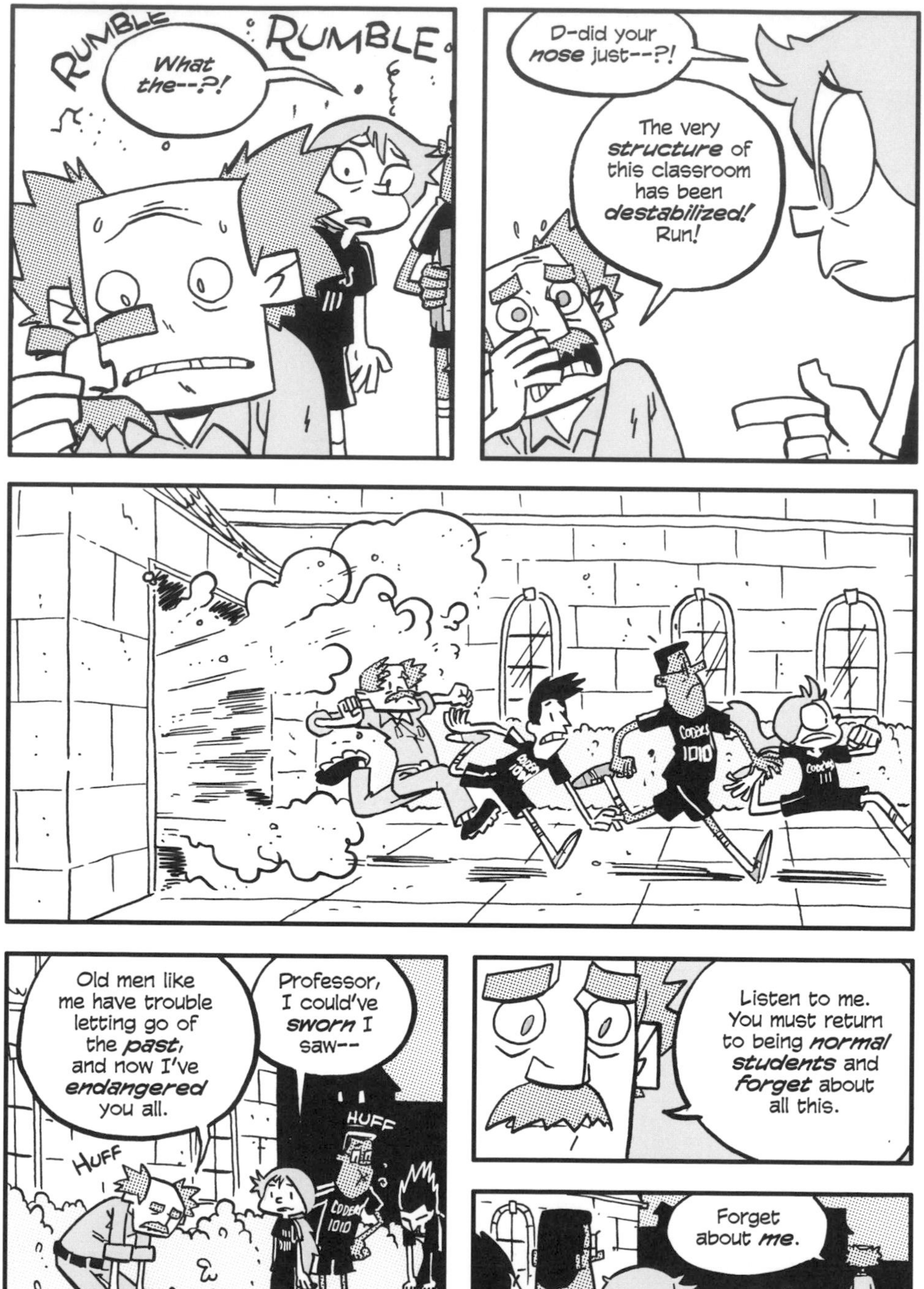

RUMBLE
RUMBLE
What the--?!
D-did your *nose* just--?!
The very *structure* of this classroom has been *destabilized!* Run!
Old men like me have trouble letting go of the *past*, and now I've *endangered* you all.
HUFF
Professor, I could've *sworn* I saw--
HUFF
Listen to me. You must return to being *normal students* and *forget* about all this.
Forget about *me*.

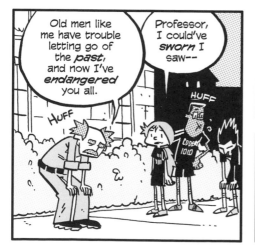

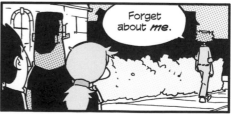

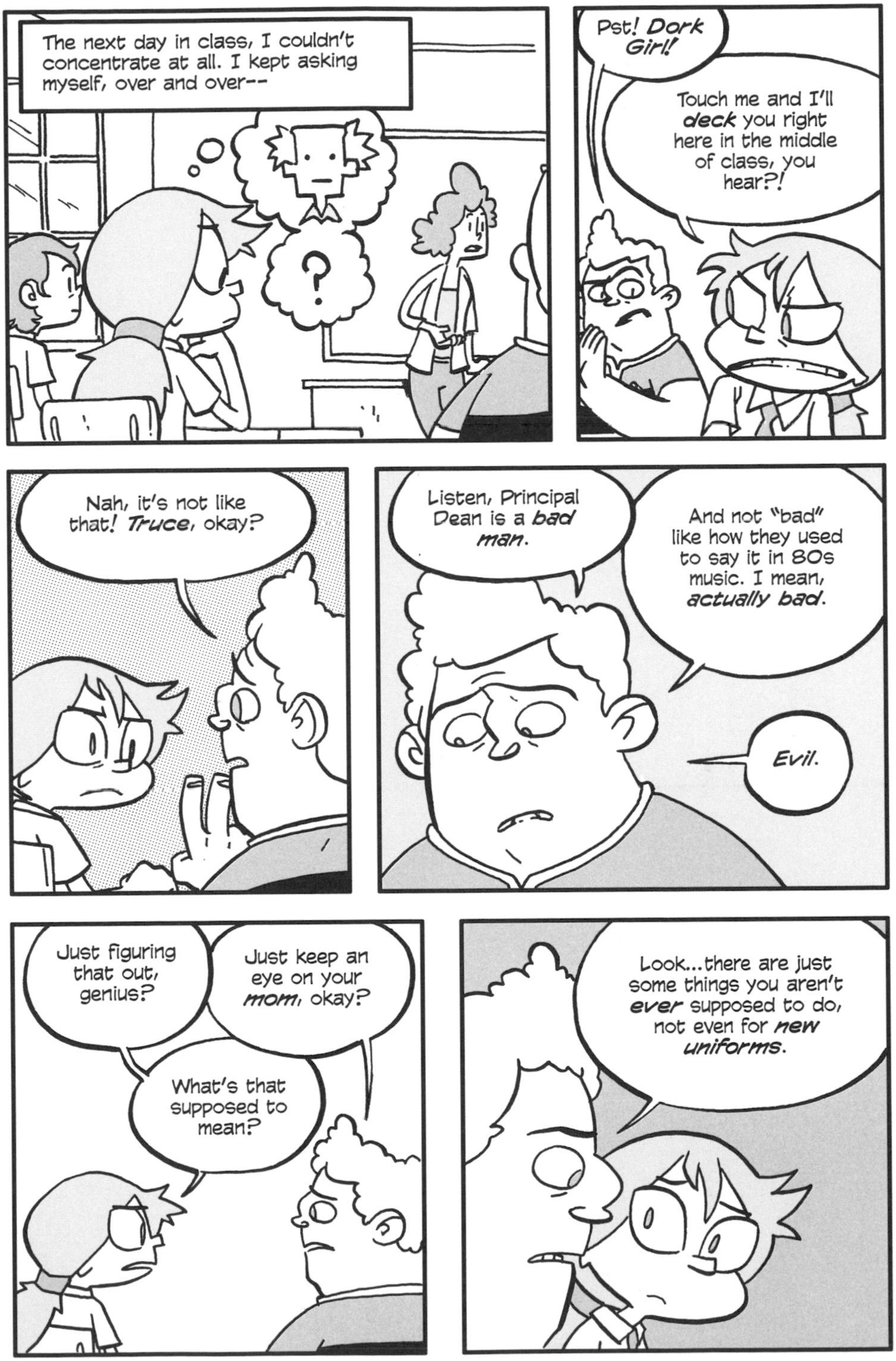
The next day in class, I couldn't concentrate at all. I kept asking myself, over and over--
?
Pst! *Dork Girl!*
Touch me and I'll ***deck*** you right here in the middle of class, you hear?!
Nah, it's not like that! *Truce*, okay?
Listen, Principal Dean is a *bad man*.
And not "bad" like how they used to say it in 80s music. I mean, ***actually bad***.
Evil.
Just figuring that out, genius?
Just keep an eye on your *mom*, okay?
What's that supposed to mean?
Look...there are just some things you aren't *ever* supposed to do, not even for *new uniforms*.

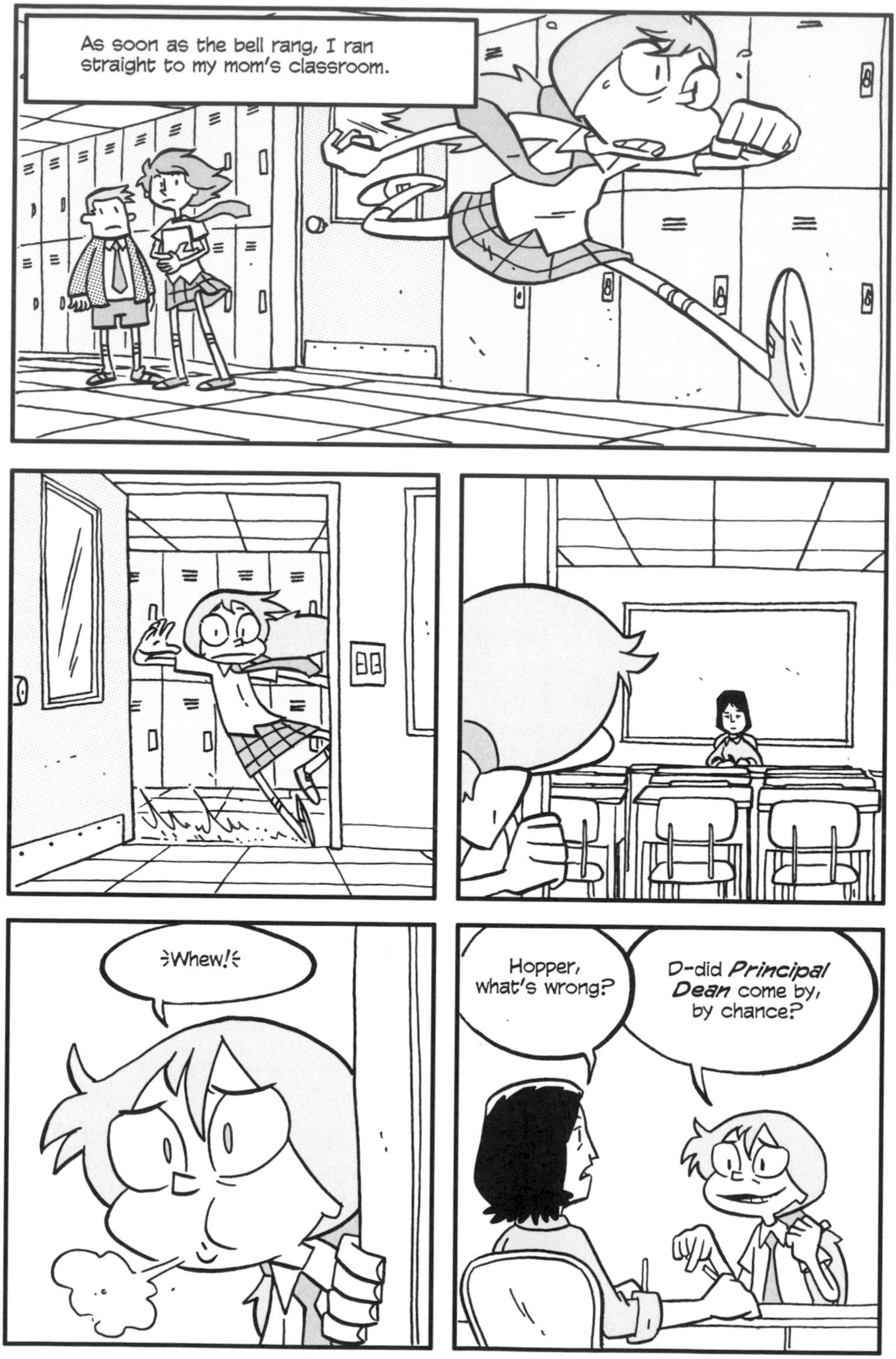
As soon as the bell rang, I ran straight to my mom's classroom.
Whew!
Hopper, what's wrong?
D-did *Principal Dean* come by, by chance?

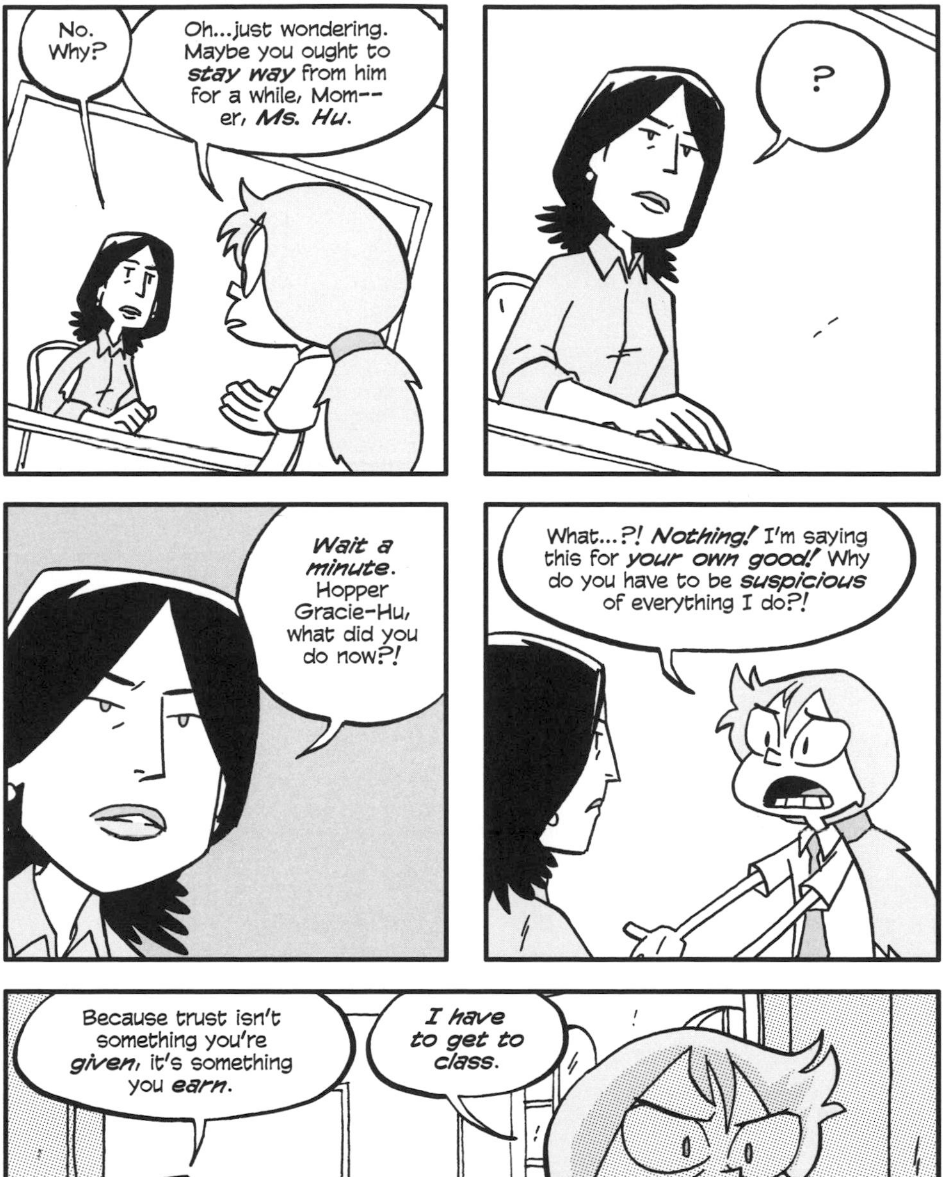
No. Why?
Oh...just wondering. Maybe you ought to *stay way* from him for a while, Mom-- er, *Ms. Hu*.
?
Wait a minute. Hopper Gracie-Hu, what did you do now?!
What...?! *Nothing!* I'm saying this for *your own good!* Why do you have to be *suspicious* of everything I do?!
Because trust isn't something you're *given*, it's something you *earn*.
I have to get to class.

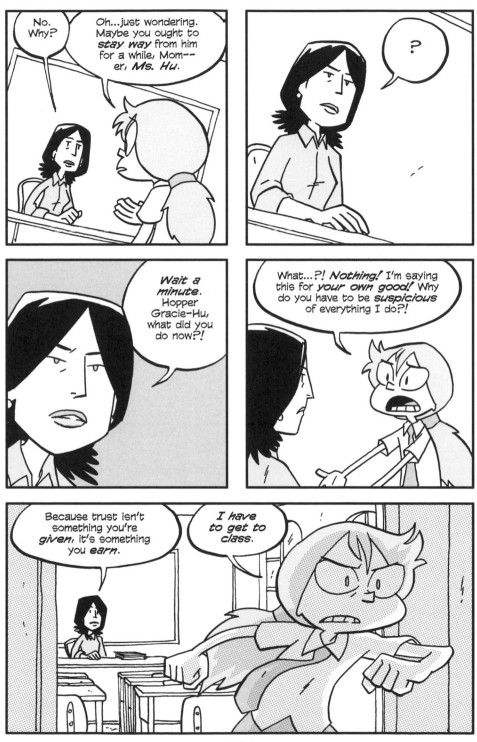

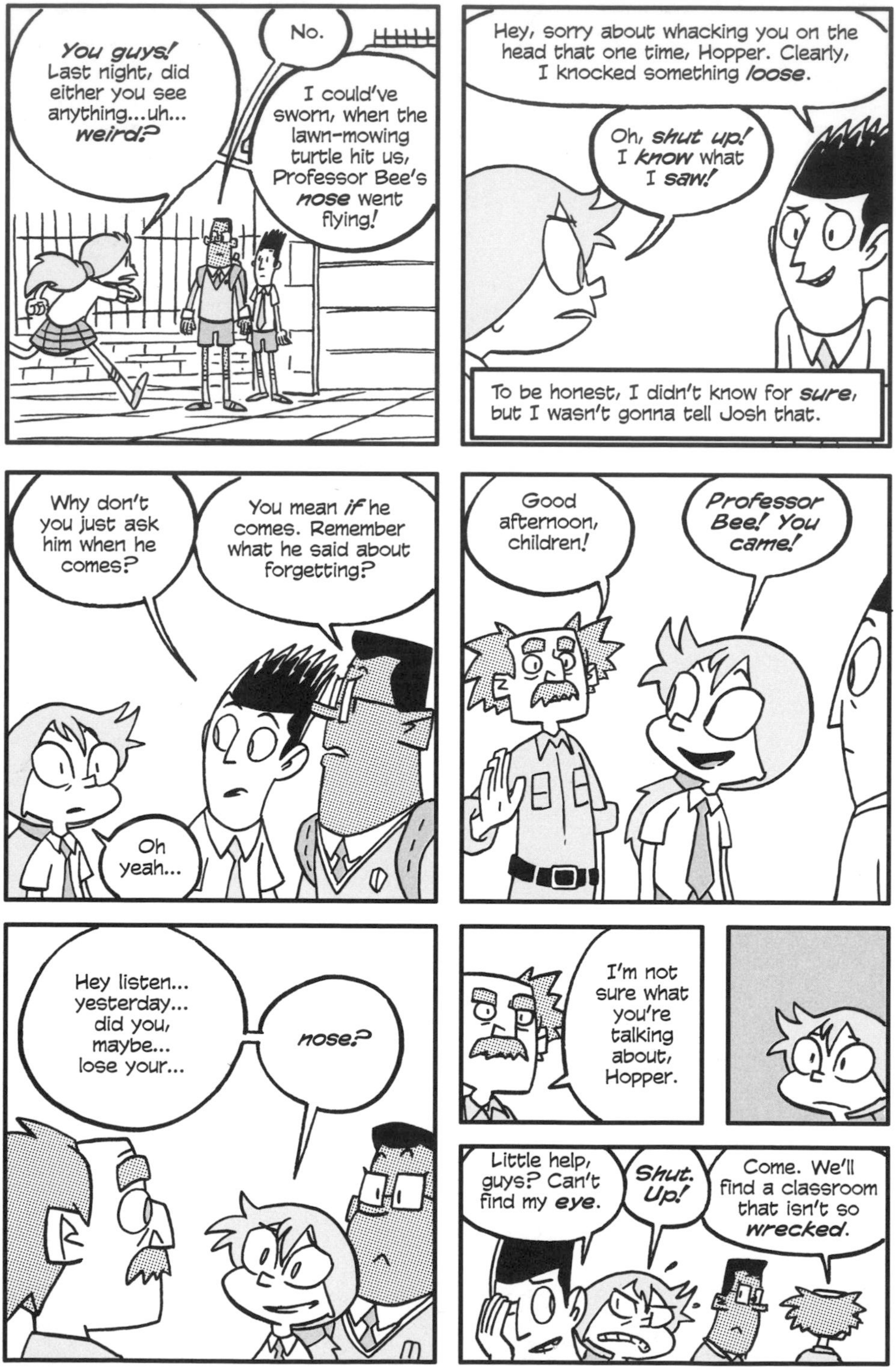
You guys! Last night, did either you see anything...uh... weird?
No.
I could've sworn, when the lawn-mowing turtle hit us, Professor Bee's nose went flying!
Hey, sorry about whacking you on the head that one time, Hopper. Clearly, I knocked something loose.
Oh, shut up! I know what I saw!
To be honest, I didn't know for sure, but I wasn't gonna tell Josh that.
Why don't you just ask him when he comes?
You mean if he comes. Remember what he said about forgetting?
Oh yeah...
Good afternoon, children!
Professor Bee! You came!
Hey listen... yesterday... did you, maybe... lose your...
nose?
I'm not sure what you're talking about, Hopper.
Little help, guys? Can't find my eye.
Shut. Up!
Come. We'll find a classroom that isn't so wrecked.

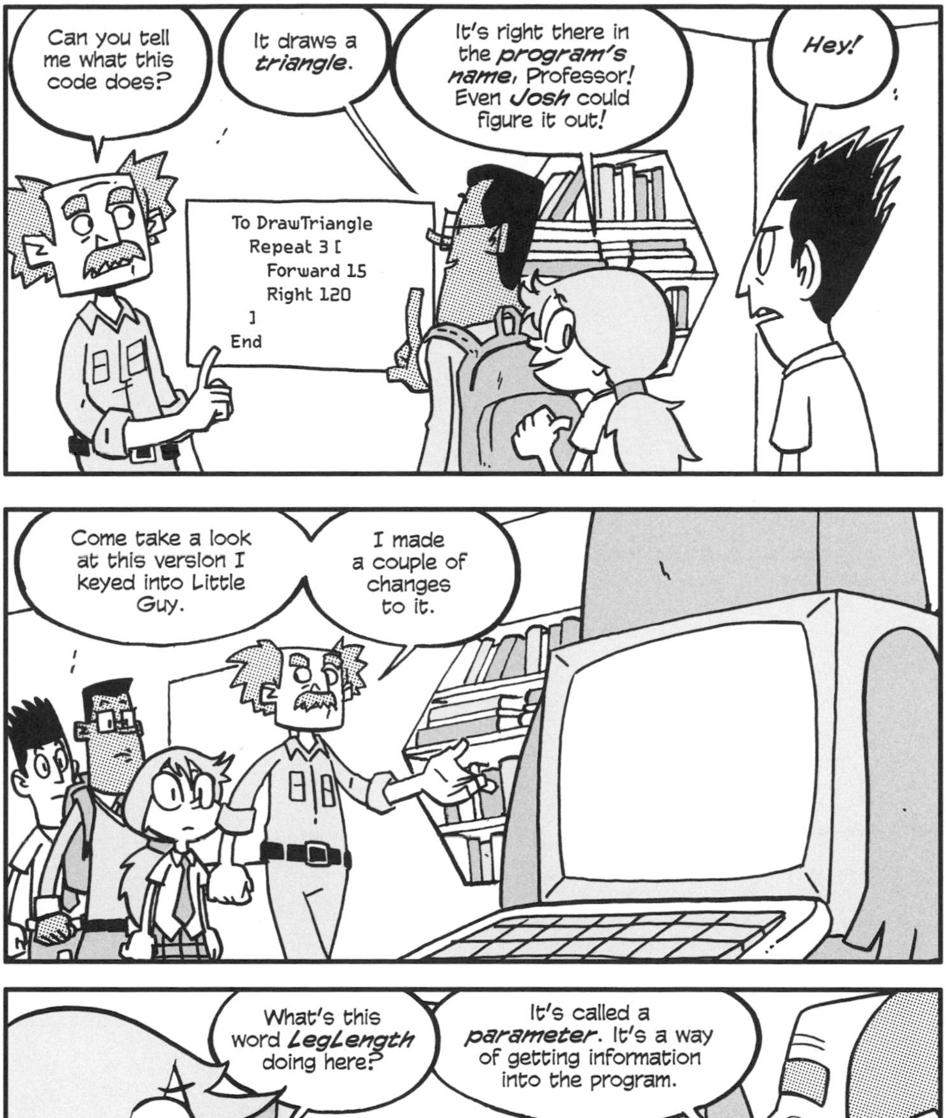
Can you tell me what this code does?
It draws a *triangle*.
It's right there in the *program's name*, Professor! Even *Josh* could figure it out!
Hey!
To DrawTriangle
Repeat 3 [
Forward 15
Right 120
]
End
Come take a look at this version I keyed into Little Guy.
I made a couple of changes to it.
What's this word *LegLength* doing here?
It's called a *parameter*. It's a way of getting information into the program.
To DrawTriangle :LegLength
Repeat 3 [
Forward :LegLength
Right 120
]
End
In this case, it lets you change the *size* of the triangle without changing any of the *code*.

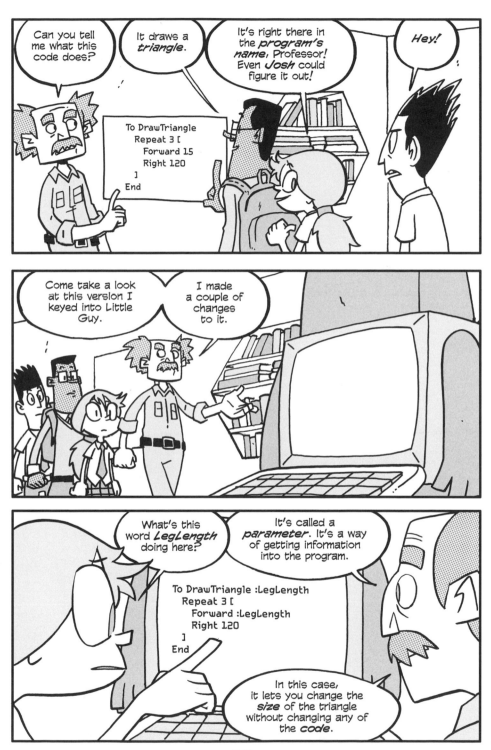

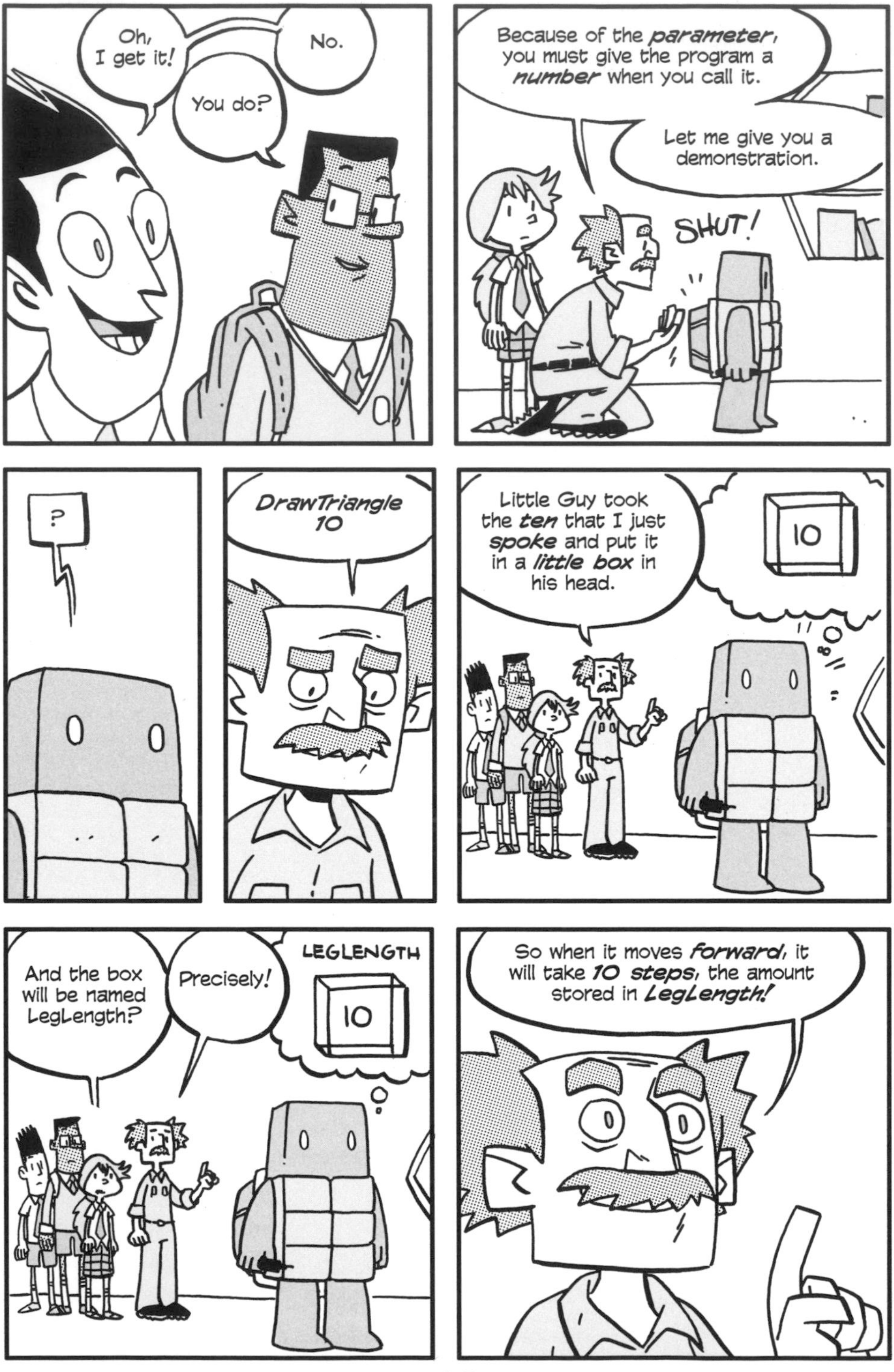

Oh, I get it!
You do?
No.
Because of the *parameter*, you must give the program a *number* when you call it.
Let me give you a demonstration.
SHUT!
?
DrawTriangle 10
Little Guy took the *ten* that I just *spoke* and put it in a *little box* in his head.
10
And the box will be named LegLength?
Precisely!
LEGLENGTH
10
So when it moves *forward*, it will take *10 steps*, the amount stored in *LegLength!*

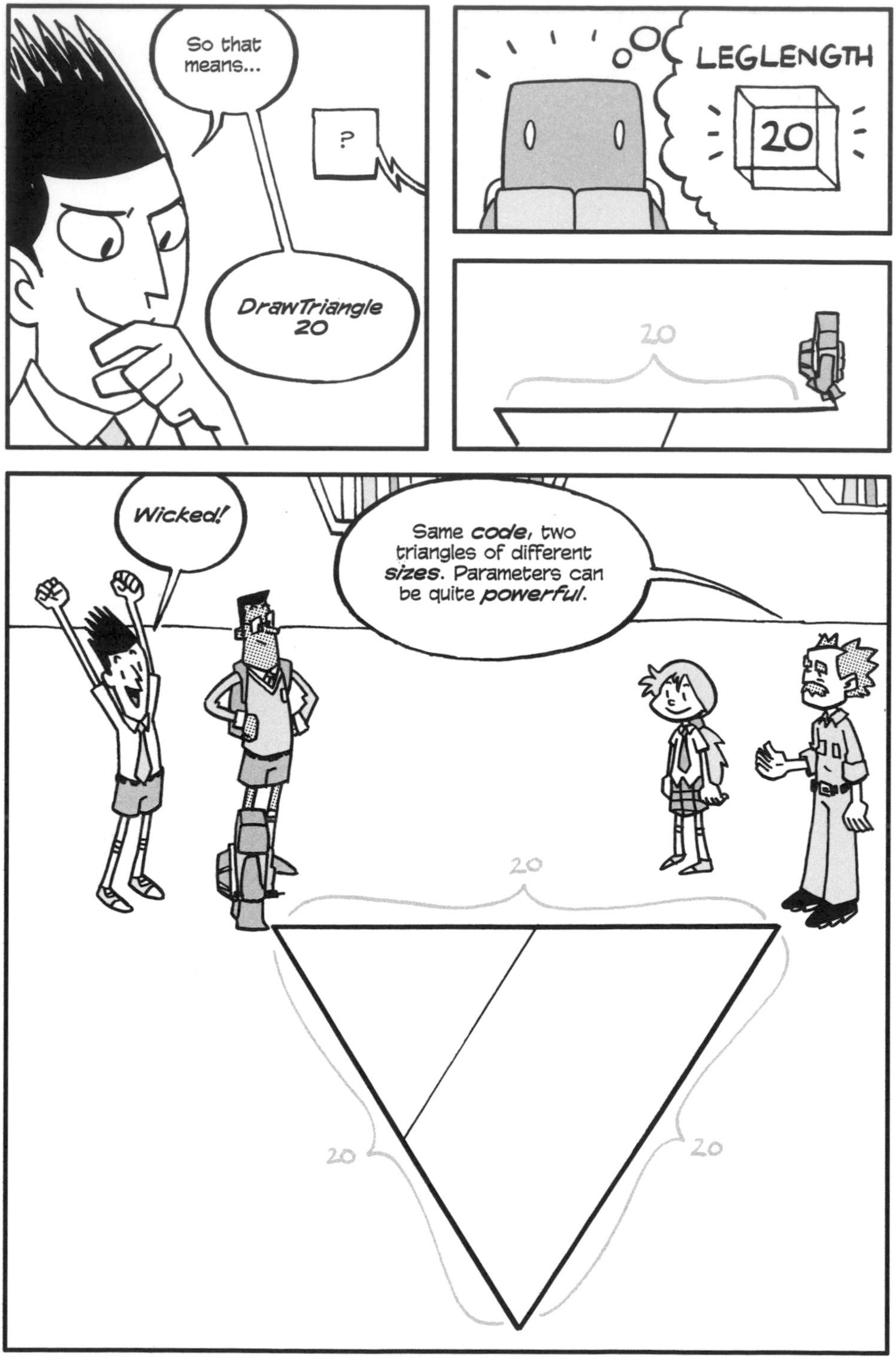

So that means...
DrawTriangle 20
?
LEGLENGTH
20
20
Wicked!
Same *code*, two triangles of different *sizes*. Parameters can be quite *powerful*.
20
20
20

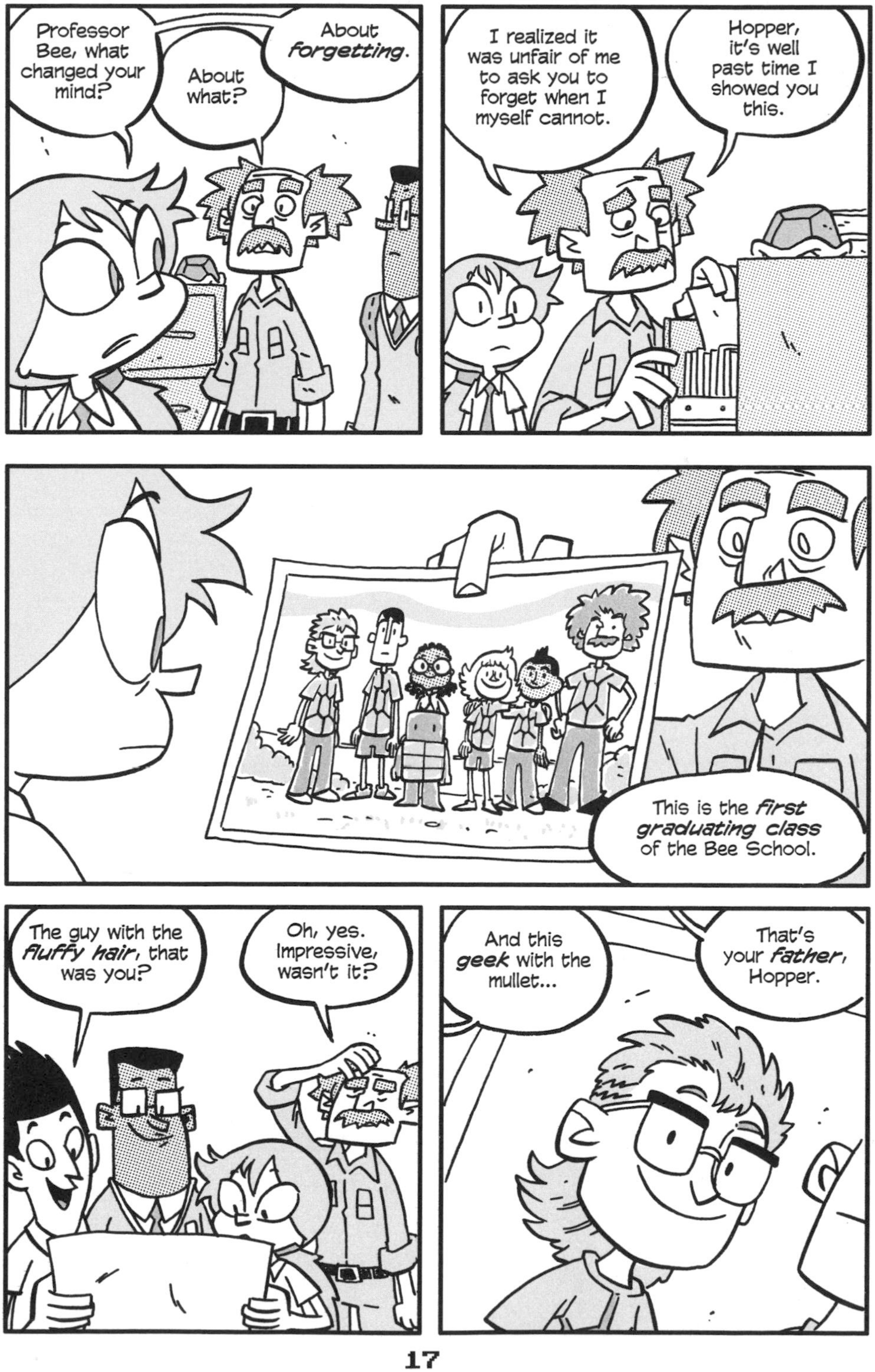
Professor Bee, what changed your mind?
About what?
About *forgetting*.
I realized it was unfair of me to ask you to forget when I myself cannot.
Hopper, it's well past time I showed you this.
This is the *first graduating class* of the Bee School.
The guy with the *fluffy hair*, that was you?
Oh, yes. Impressive, wasn't it?
And this *geek* with the mullet...
That's your *father*, Hopper.

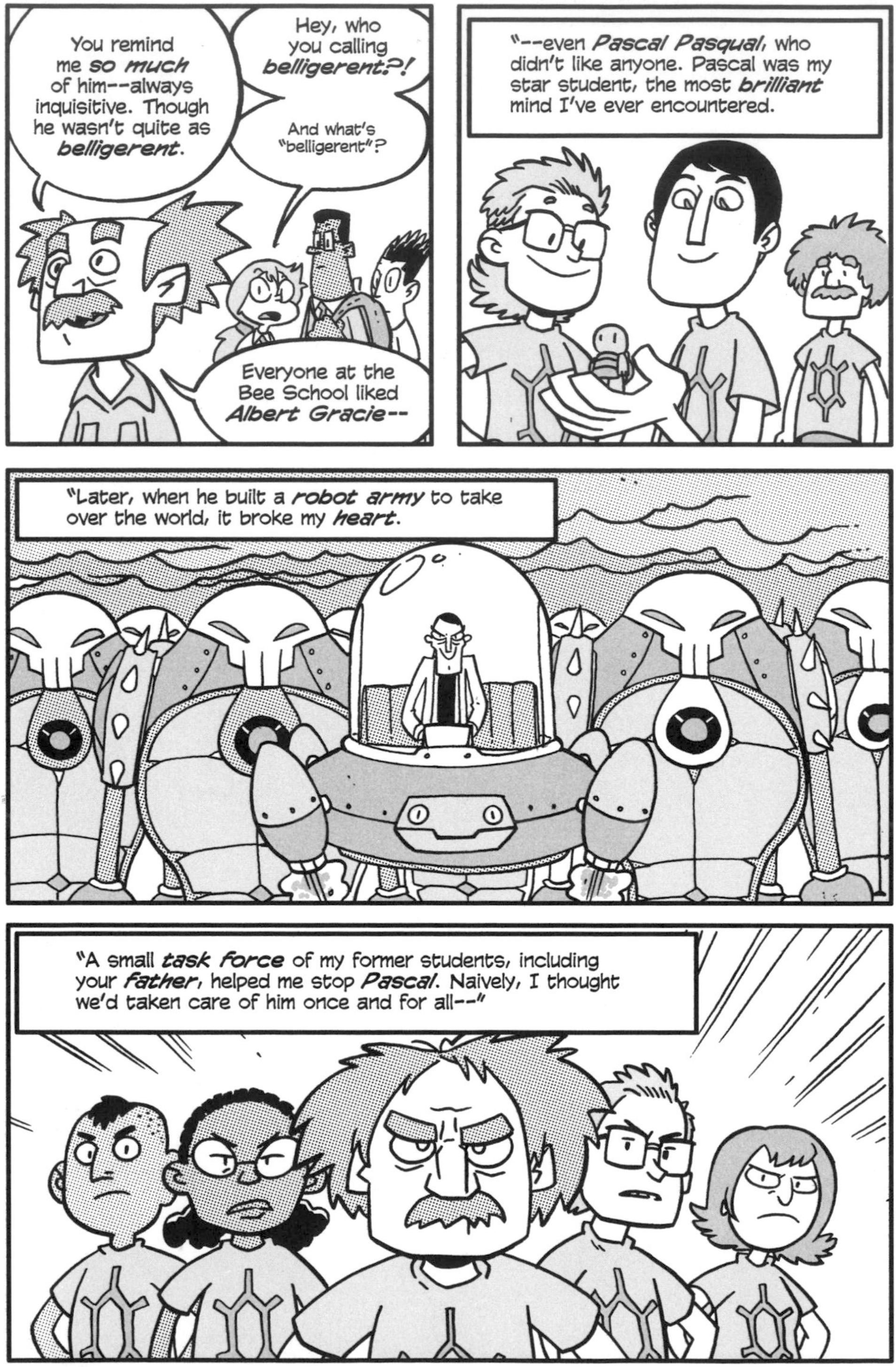
You remind me so much of him--always inquisitive. Though he wasn't quite as belligerent.
Hey, who you calling belligerent?!
And what's "belligerent"?
Everyone at the Bee School liked Albert Gracie--
"--even Pascal Pasqual, who didn't like anyone. Pascal was my star student, the most brilliant mind I've ever encountered.
"Later, when he built a robot army to take over the world, it broke my heart.
"A small task force of my former students, including your father, helped me stop Pascal. Naively, I thought we'd taken care of him once and for all--"

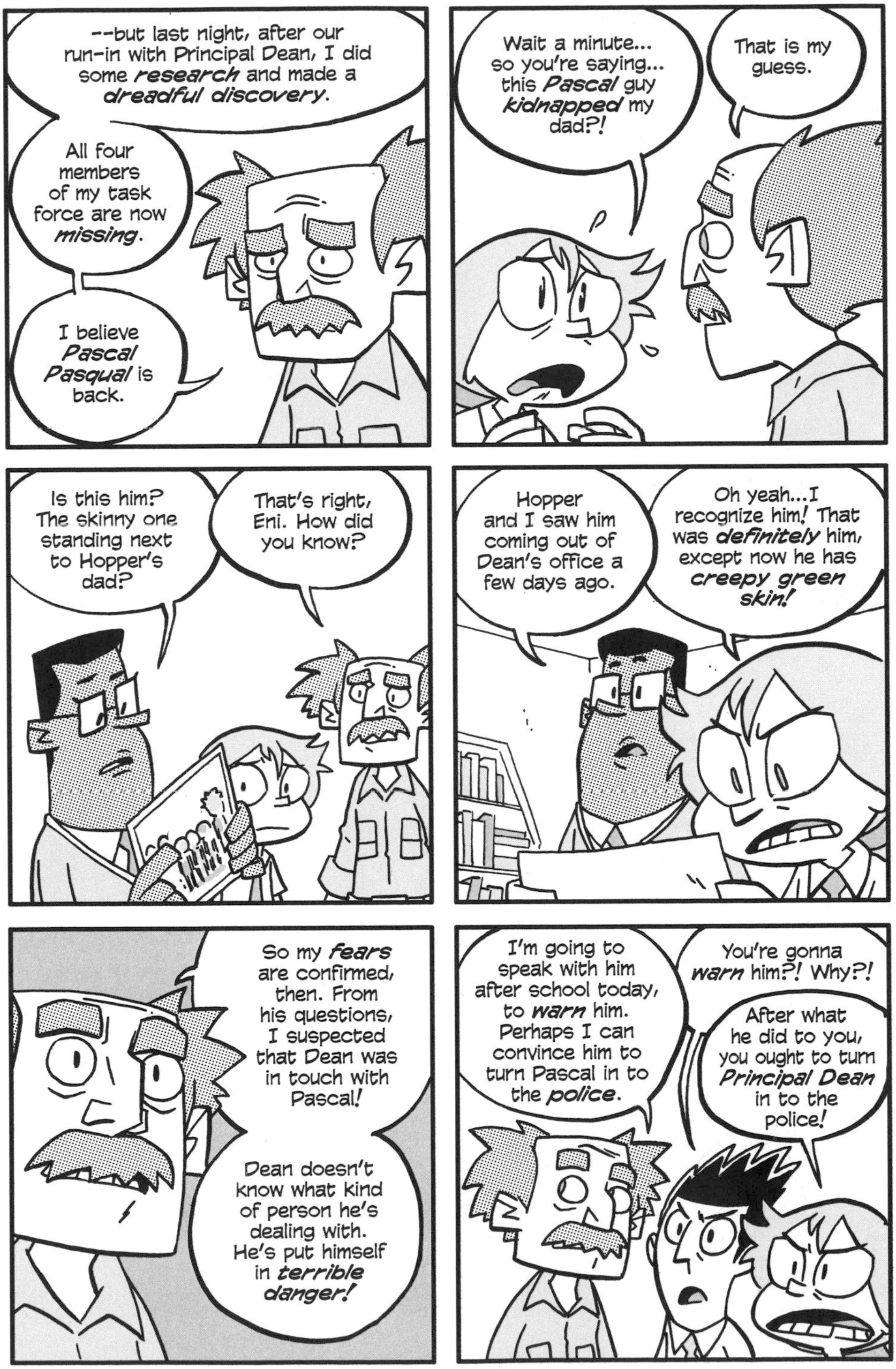
--but last night, after our run-in with Principal Dean, I did some *research* and made a *dreadful discovery*.
All four members of my task force are now *missing*.
I believe *Pascal Pasqual* is back.
Wait a minute... so you're saying... this *Pascal* guy *kidnapped* my dad?!
That is my guess.
Is this him? The skinny one standing next to Hopper's dad?
That's right, Eni. How did you know?
Hopper and I saw him coming out of Dean's office a few days ago.
Oh yeah...I recognize him! That was *definitely* him, except now he has *creepy green skin!*
So my *fears* are confirmed, then. From his questions, I suspected that Dean was in touch with Pascal!
Dean doesn't know what kind of person he's dealing with. He's put himself in *terrible danger!*
I'm going to speak with him after school today, to *warn* him. Perhaps I can convince him to turn Pascal in to the *police*.
You're gonna *warn* him?! Why?!
After what he did to you, you ought to turn *Principal Dean* in to the police!

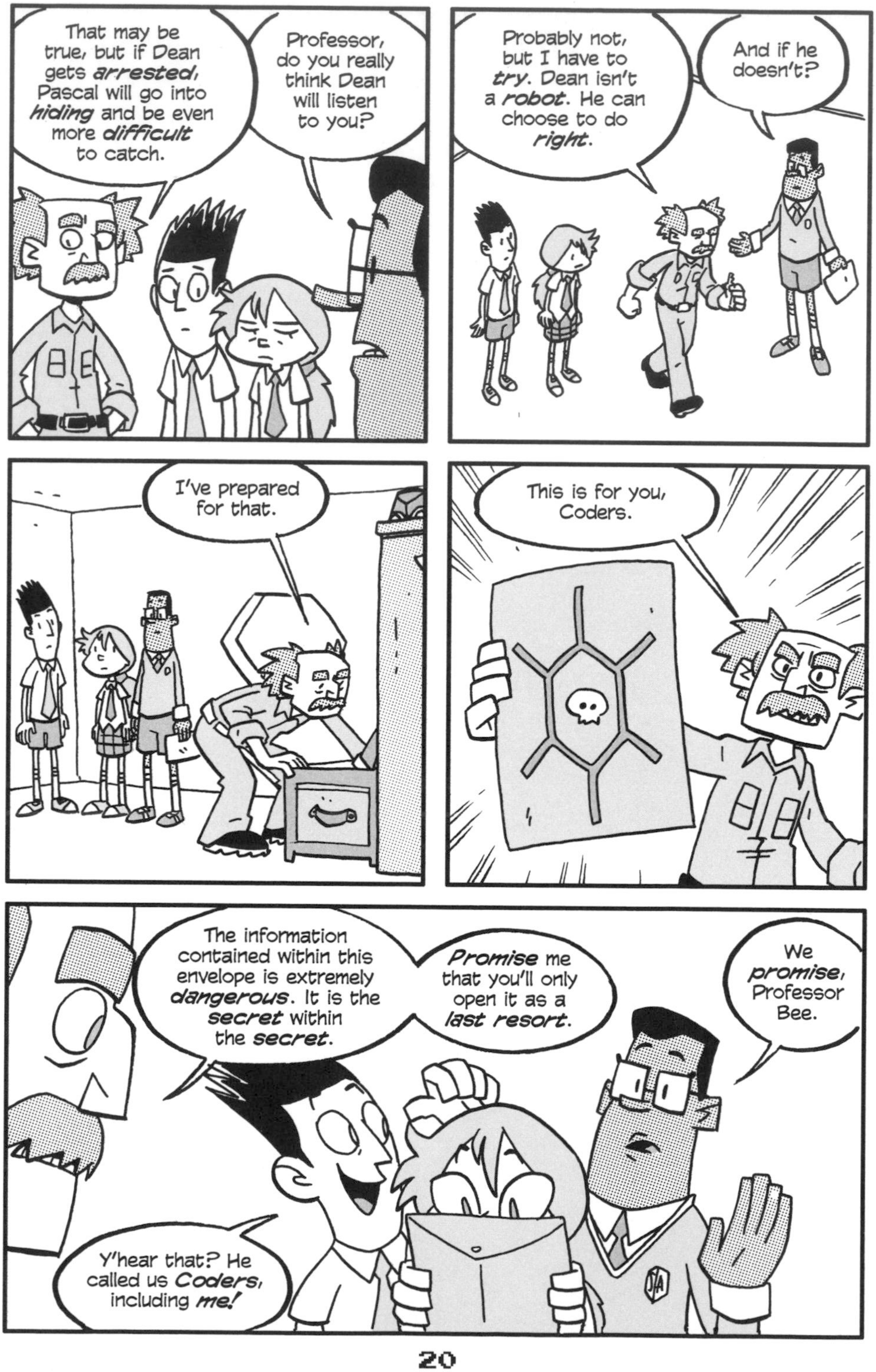
That may be true, but if Dean gets *arrested*, Pascal will go into *hiding* and be even more *difficult* to catch.
Professor, do you really think Dean will listen to you?
Probably not, but I have to *try*. Dean isn't a *robot*. He can choose to do *right*.
And if he doesn't?
I've prepared for that.
This is for you, Coders.
The information contained within this envelope is extremely *dangerous*. It is the *secret* within the *secret*.
Promise me that you'll only open it as a *last resort*.
We *promise*, Professor Bee.
Y'hear that? He called us *Coders*, including *me!*

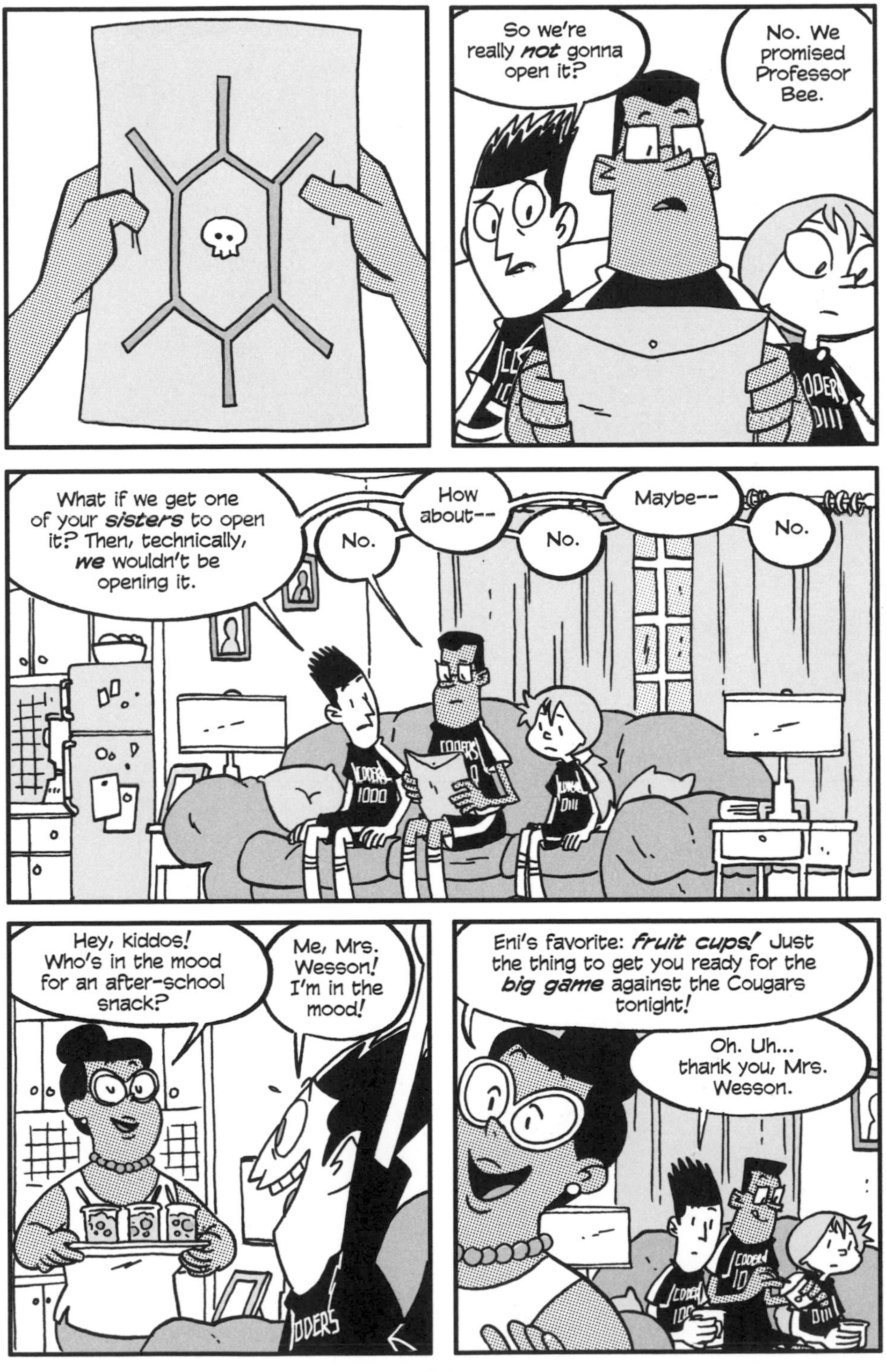
So we're really *not* gonna open it?
No. We promised Professor Bee.
What if we get one of your *sisters* to open it? Then, technically, *we* wouldn't be opening it.
No.
How about--
No.
Maybe--
No.
Hey, kiddos! Who's in the mood for an after-school snack?
Me, Mrs. Wesson! I'm in the mood!
Eni's favorite: *fruit cups!* Just the thing to get you ready for the *big game* against the Cougars tonight!
Oh. Uh... thank you, Mrs. Wesson.

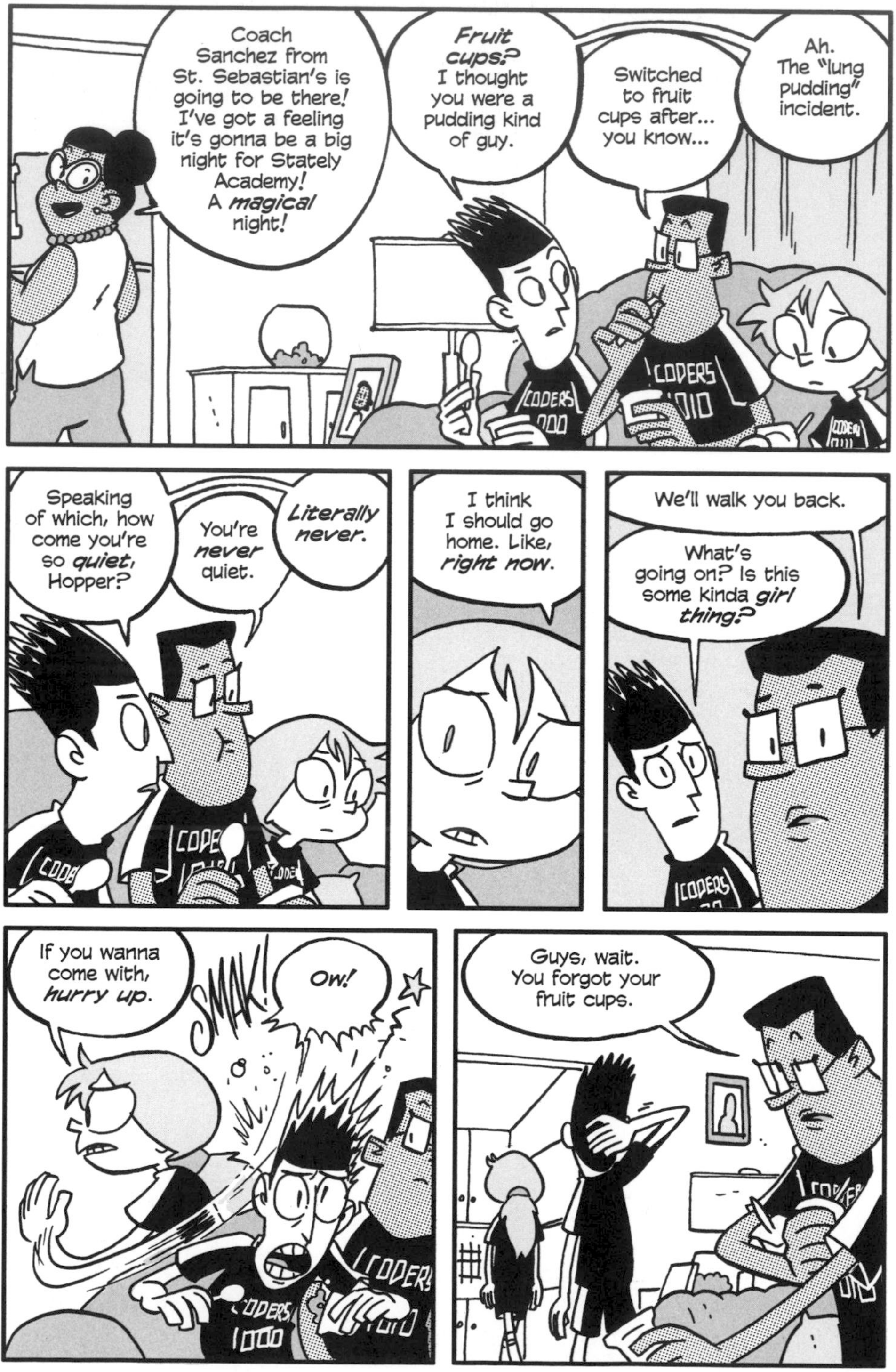
Coach Sanchez from St. Sebastian's is going to be there! I've got a feeling it's gonna be a big night for Stately Academy! A *magical* night!
Fruit cups? I thought you were a pudding kind of guy.
Switched to fruit cups after... you know...
Ah. The "lung pudding" incident.
CODERS 1010
Speaking of which, how come you're so *quiet*, Hopper?
You're *never* quiet.
Literally never.
I think I should go home. Like, *right now*.
We'll walk you back.
What's going on? Is this some kinda *girl thing?*
If you wanna come with, *hurry up*.
SMAK!
Ow!
CODERS 1000
Guys, wait. You forgot your fruit cups.

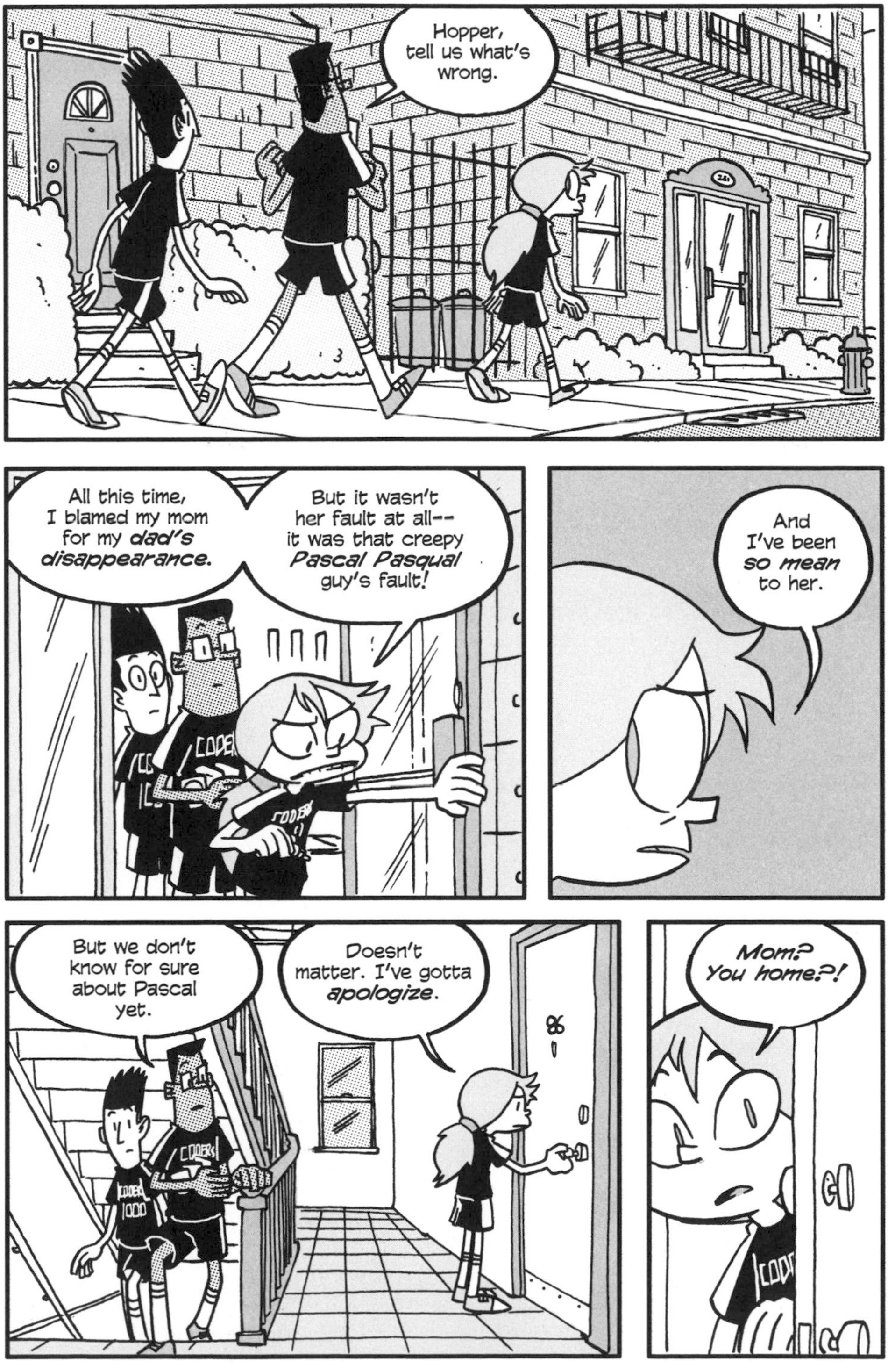
Hopper, tell us what's wrong.
All this time, I blamed my mom for my *dad's disappearance.*
But it wasn't her fault at all-- it was that creepy *Pascal Pasqual* guy's fault!
And I've been *so mean* to her.
But we don't know for sure about Pascal yet.
Doesn't matter. I've gotta *apologize*.
Mom? You home?!

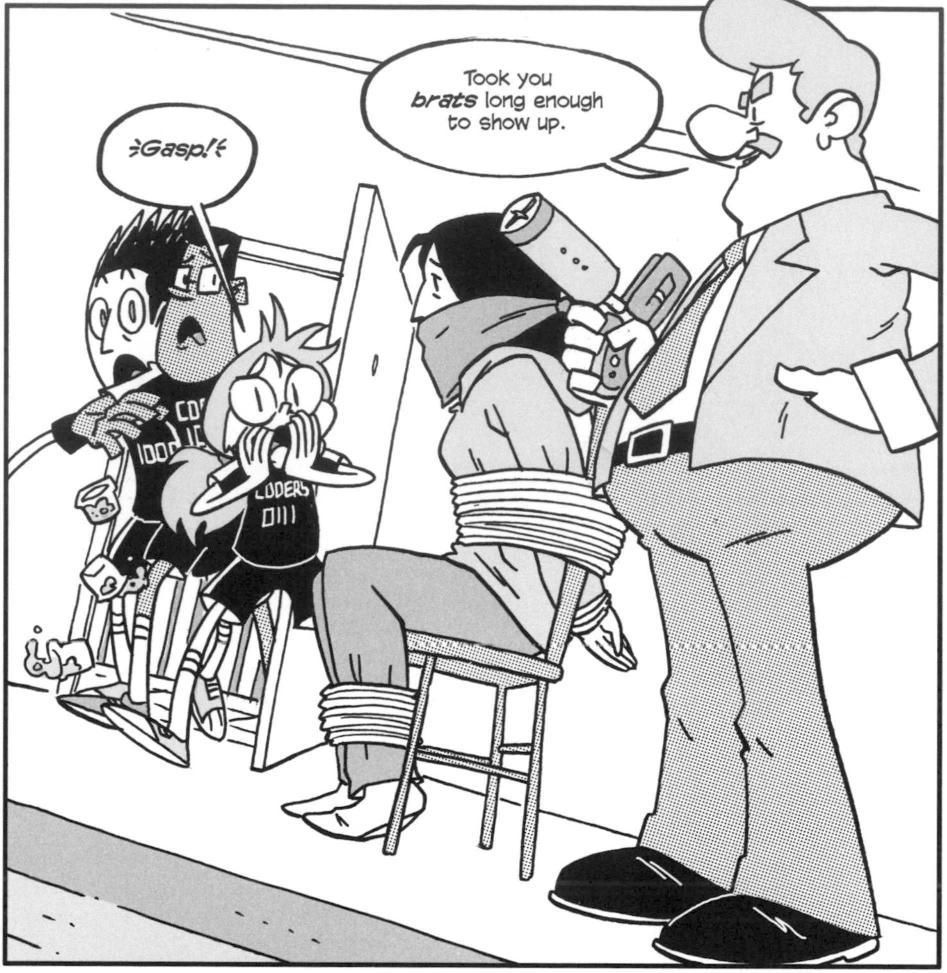
Took you **brats** long enough to show up.
Gasp!

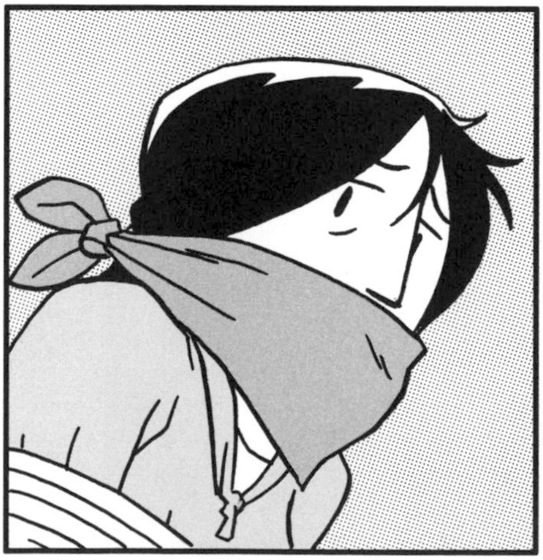

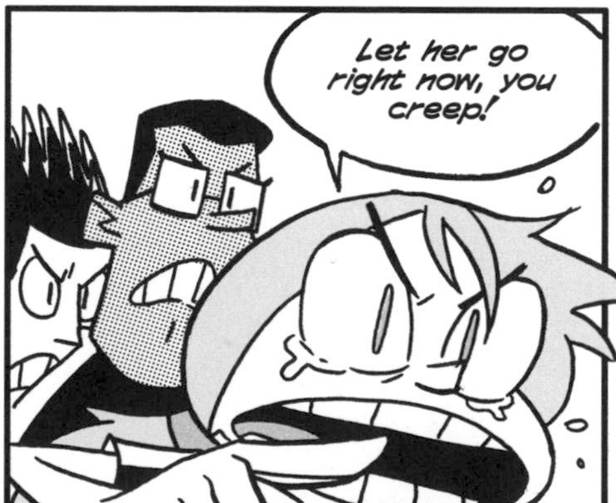
Let her go right now, you creep!

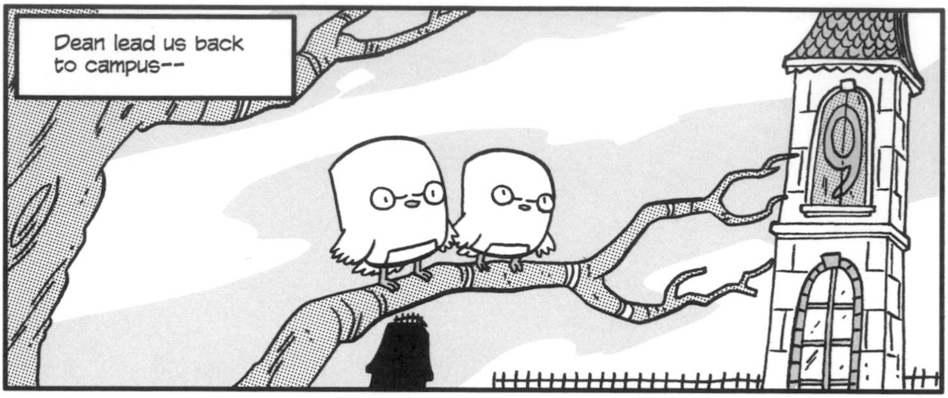
Dean lead us back to campus--

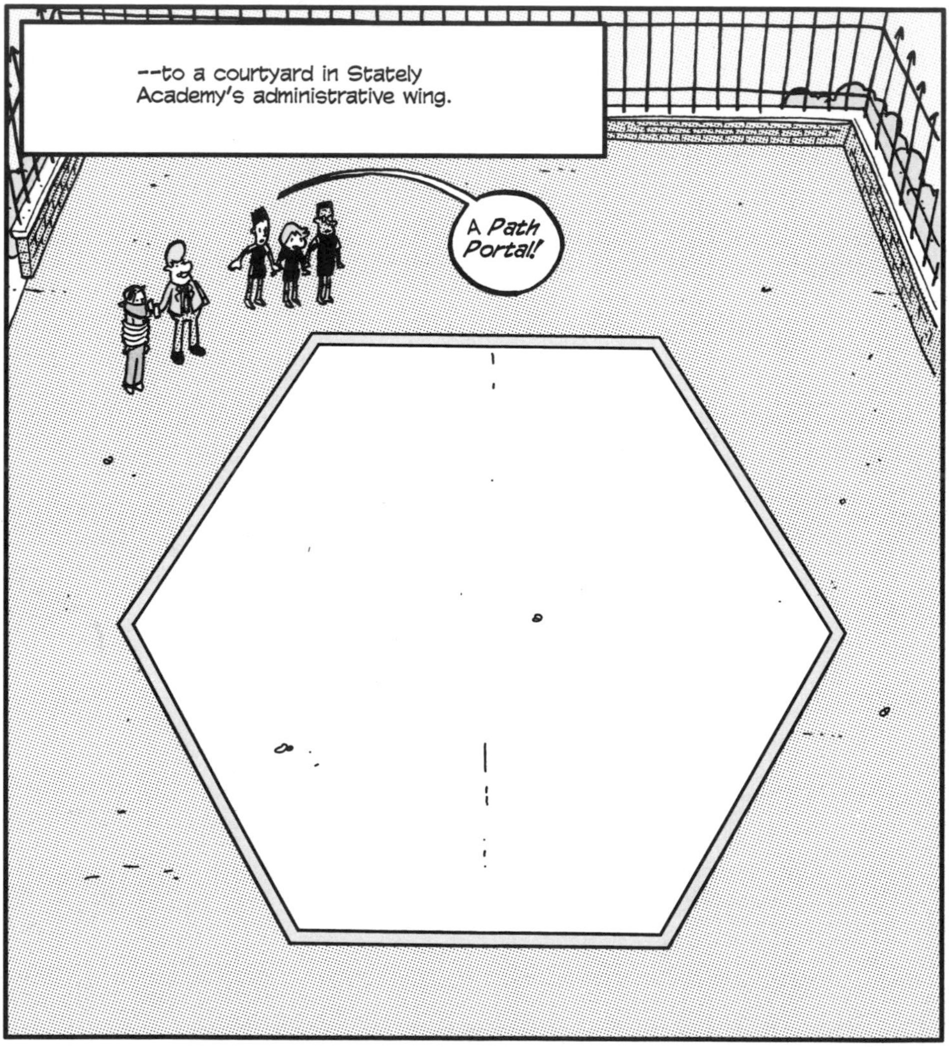
--to a courtyard in Stately Academy's administrative wing.
A *Path Portal!*

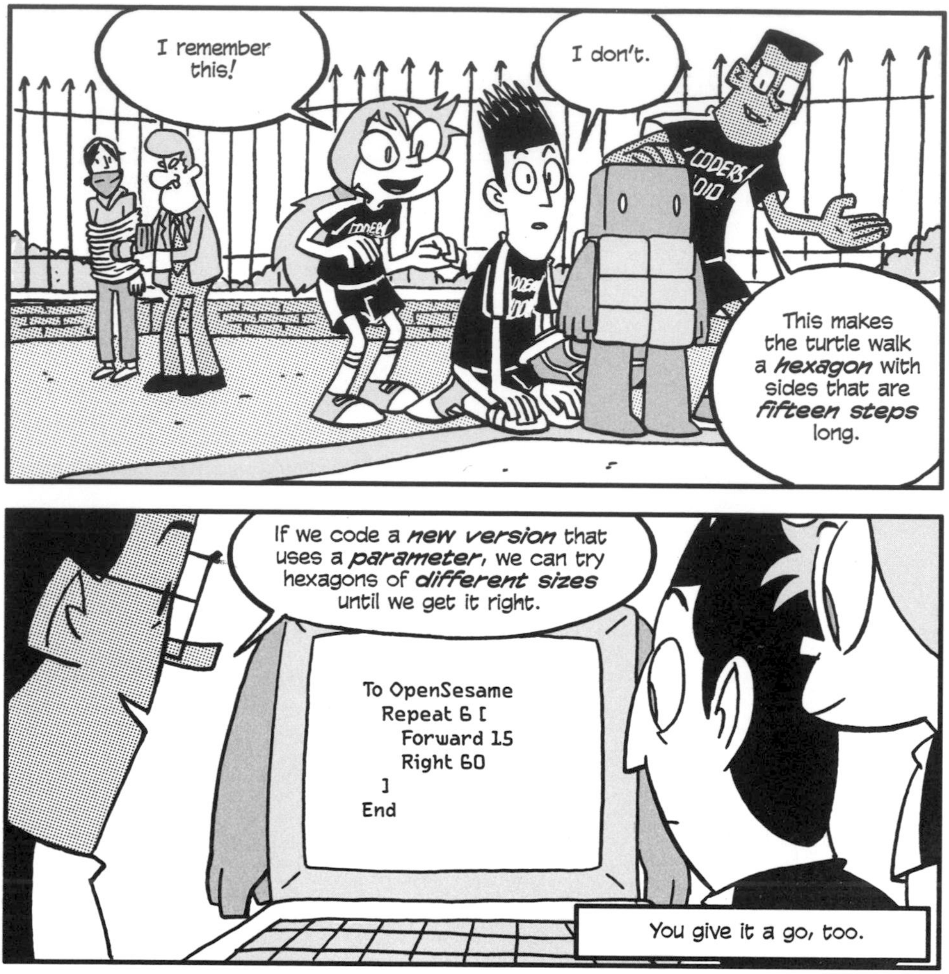
I remember this!
I don't.
This makes the turtle walk a ***hexagon*** with sides that are ***fifteen steps*** long.
If we code a ***new version*** that uses a ***parameter***, we can try hexagons of ***different sizes*** until we get it right.
To OpenSesame
Repeat 6 [
Forward 15
Right 60
]
End
You give it a go, too.
Good thinking, Eni! ***Let's do this!***
Can you write a program that uses a parameter to walk a hexagon?

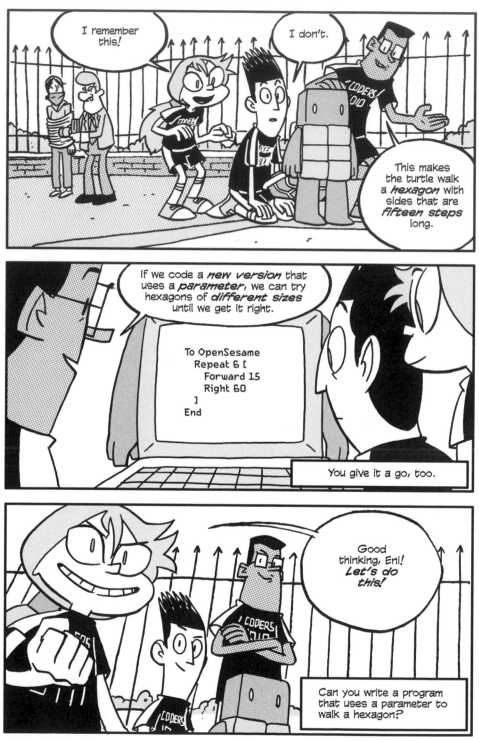

Chapter

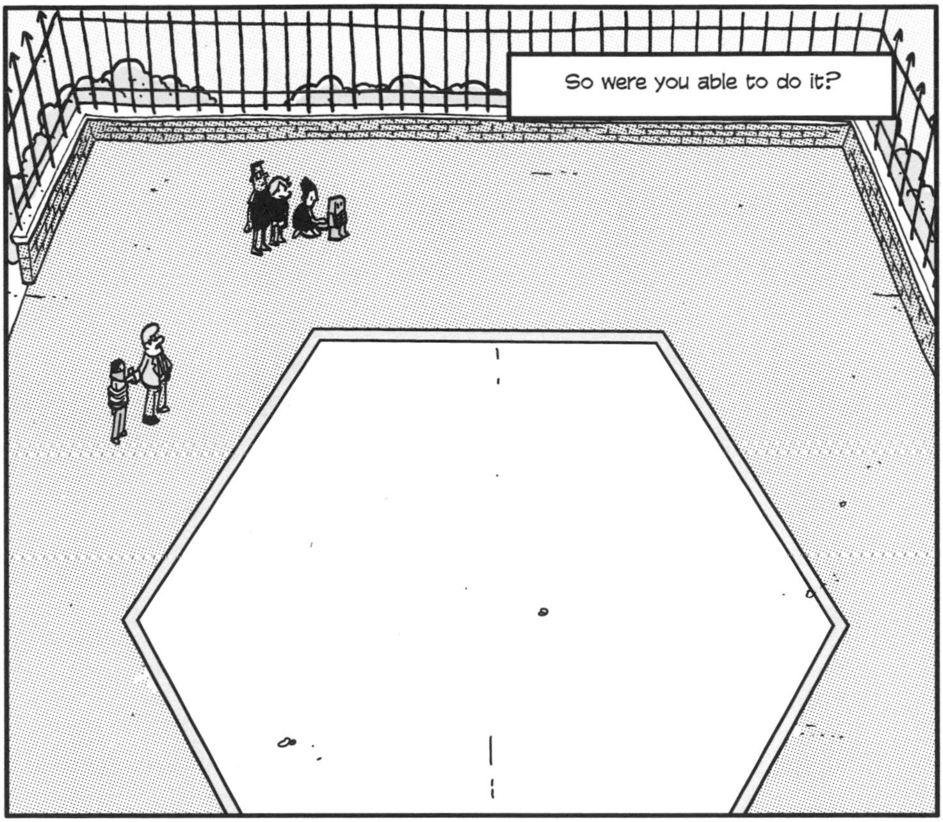
So were you able to do it?

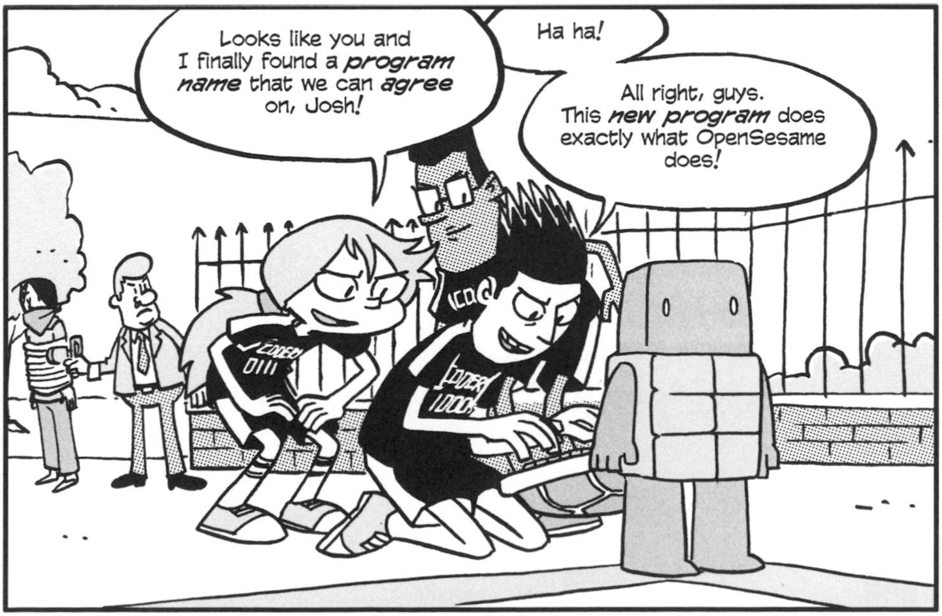
Looks like you and I finally found a ***program name*** that we can ***agree*** on, Josh!
Ha ha!
All right, guys. This ***new program*** does exactly what OpenSesame does!

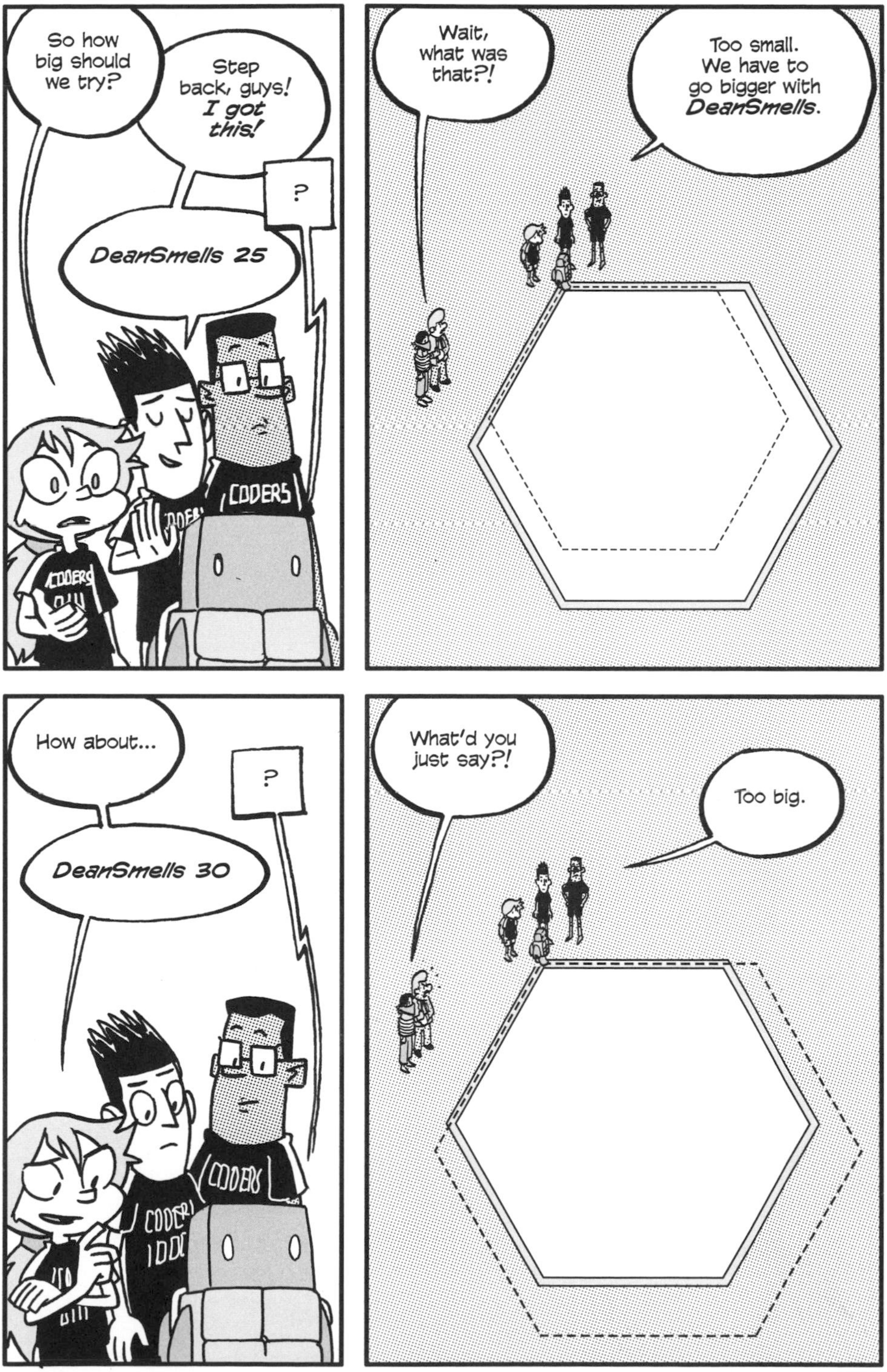
So how big should we try?
Step back, guys! *I got this!*
?
DeanSmells 25
Wait, what was that?!
Too small. We have to go bigger with *DeanSmells*.
How about...
?
DeanSmells 30
What'd you just say?!
Too big.

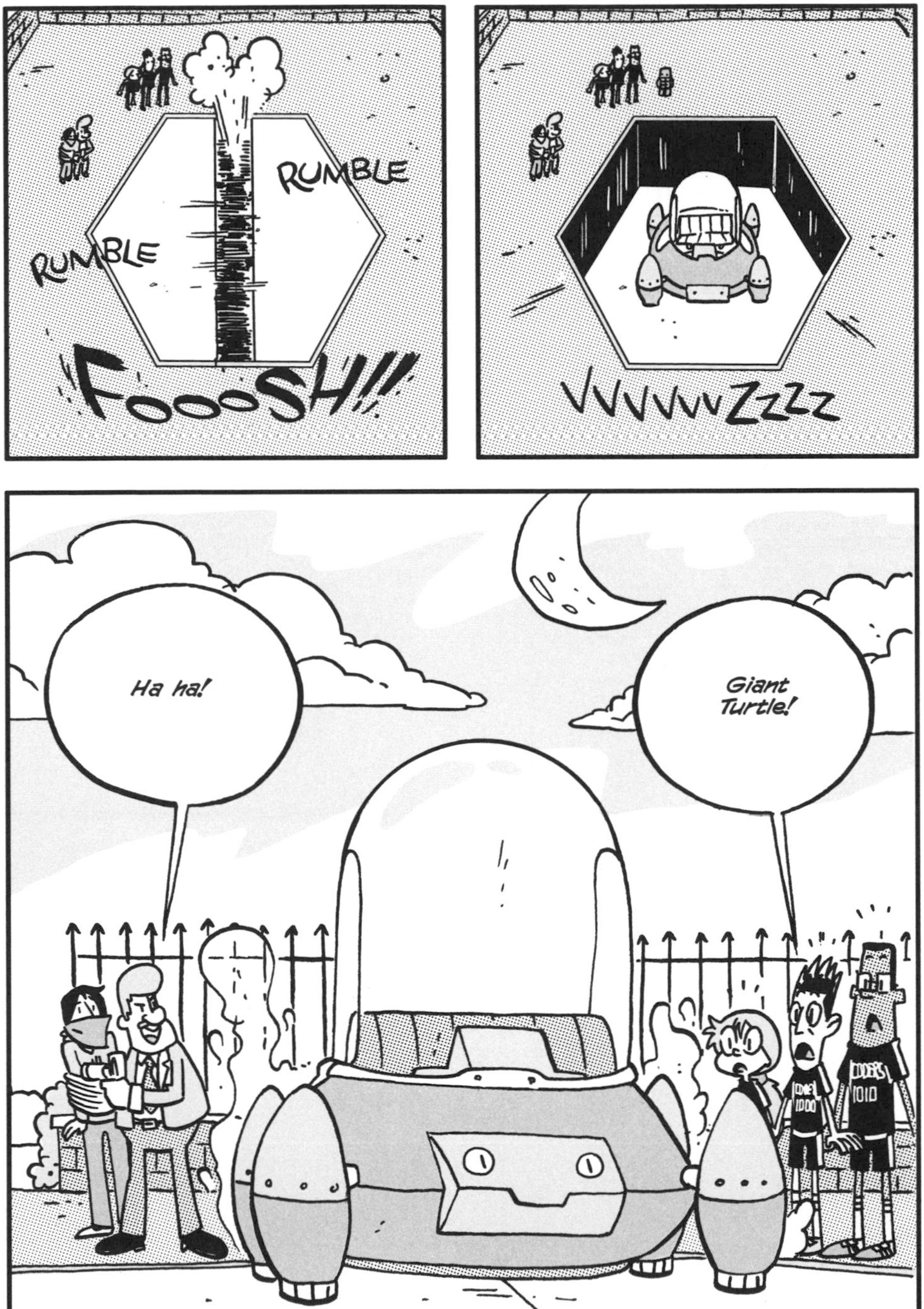

RUMBLE
RUMBLE
FOOOSH!!
VVVVVVVZzzz
Ha ha!
Giant Turtle!

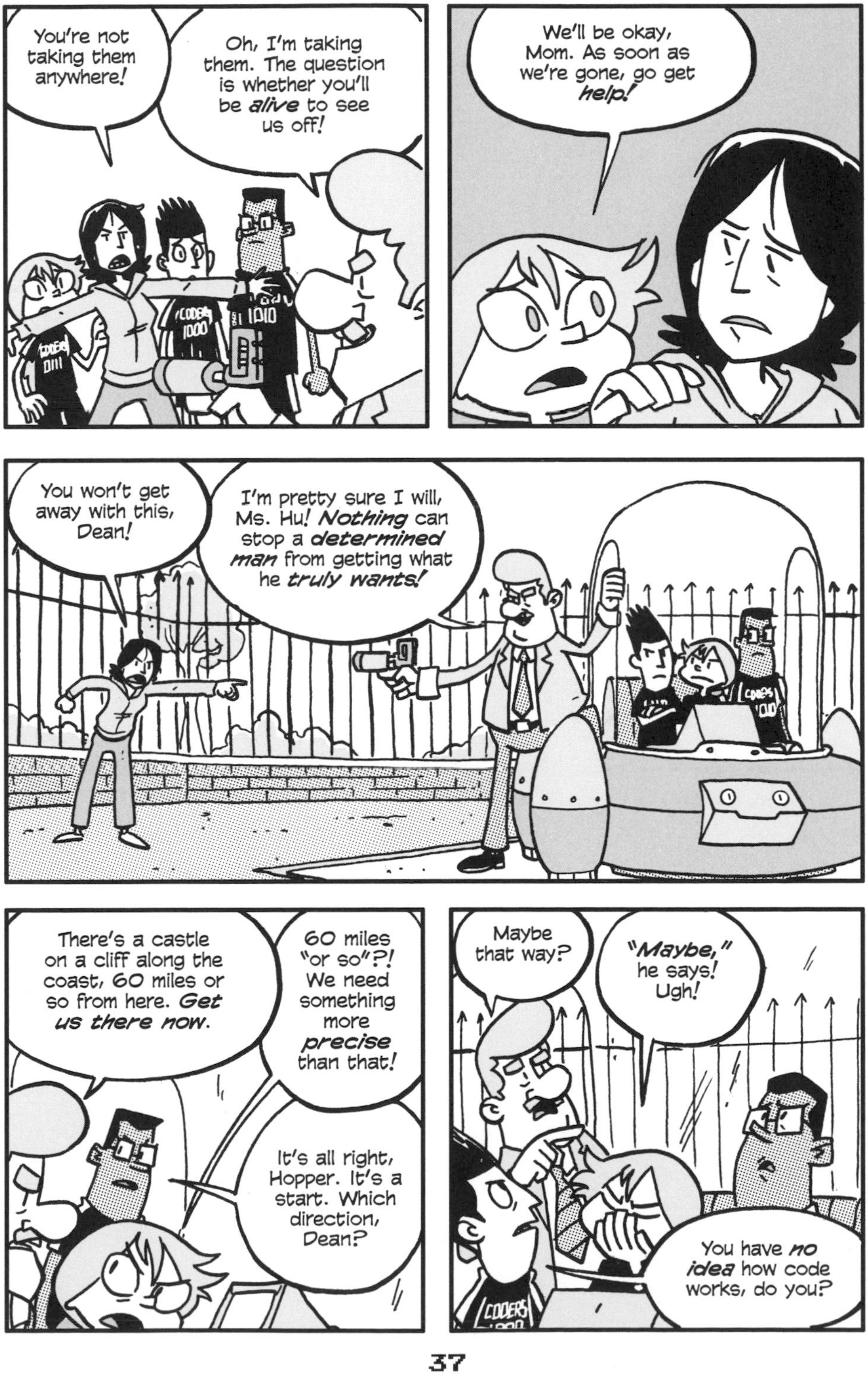

You're not taking them anywhere!
Oh, I'm taking them. The question is whether you'll be *alive* to see us off!
CODERS 1000
CODERS 1010
We'll be okay, Mom. As soon as we're gone, go get *help!*
You won't get away with this, Dean!
I'm pretty sure I will, Ms. Hu! *Nothing* can stop a *determined man* from getting what he *truly wants!*
There's a castle on a cliff along the coast, 60 miles or so from here. *Get us there now*.
60 miles "or so"?! We need something more *precise* than that!
It's all right, Hopper. It's a start. Which direction, Dean?
Maybe that way?
"Maybe," he says! Ugh!
You have *no idea* how code works, do you?

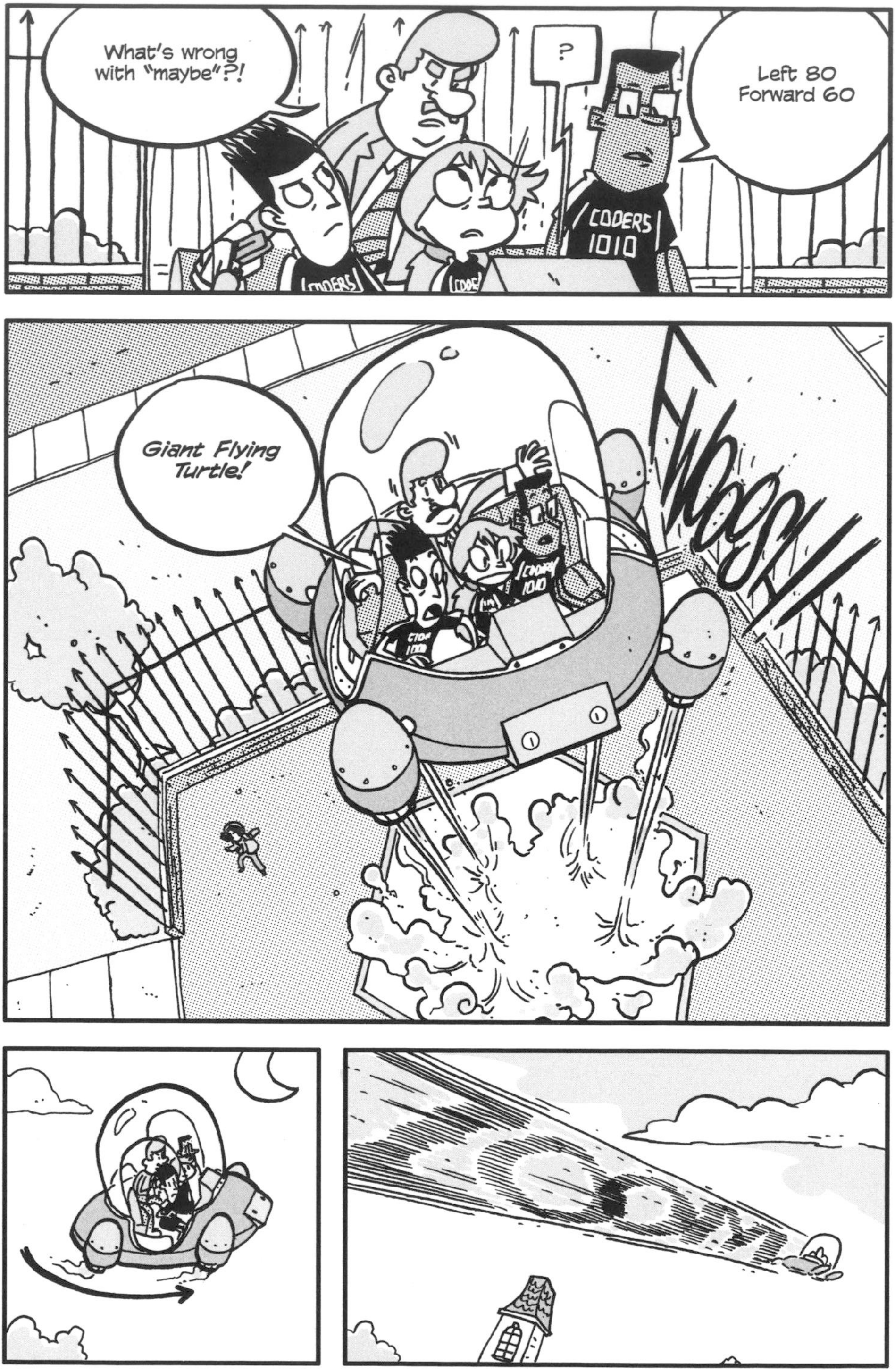
What's wrong with "maybe"?!
?
Left 80 Forward 60
CODERS 1010
Giant Flying Turtle!
FWOOSH!!

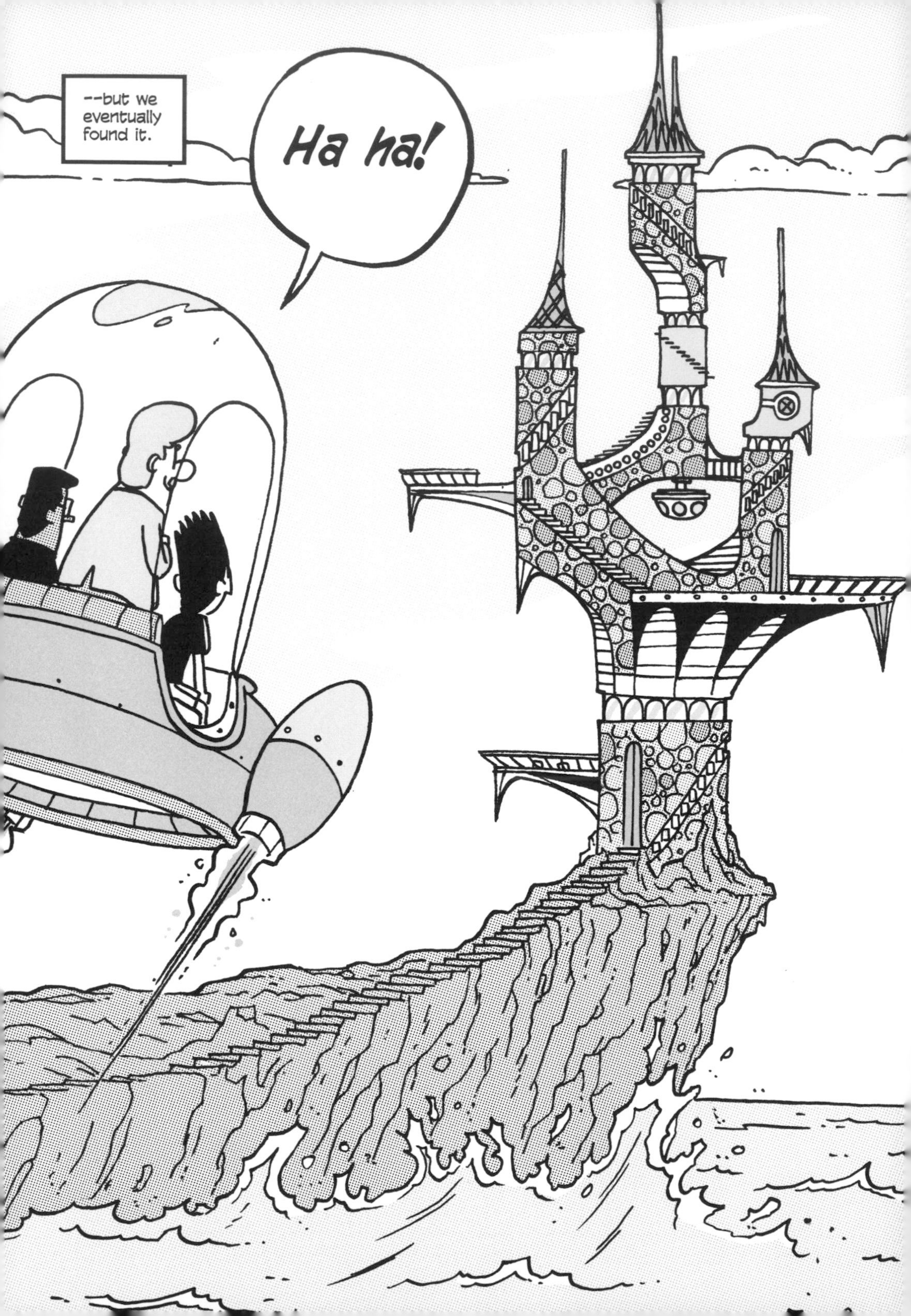
--but we eventually found it.
Ha ha!

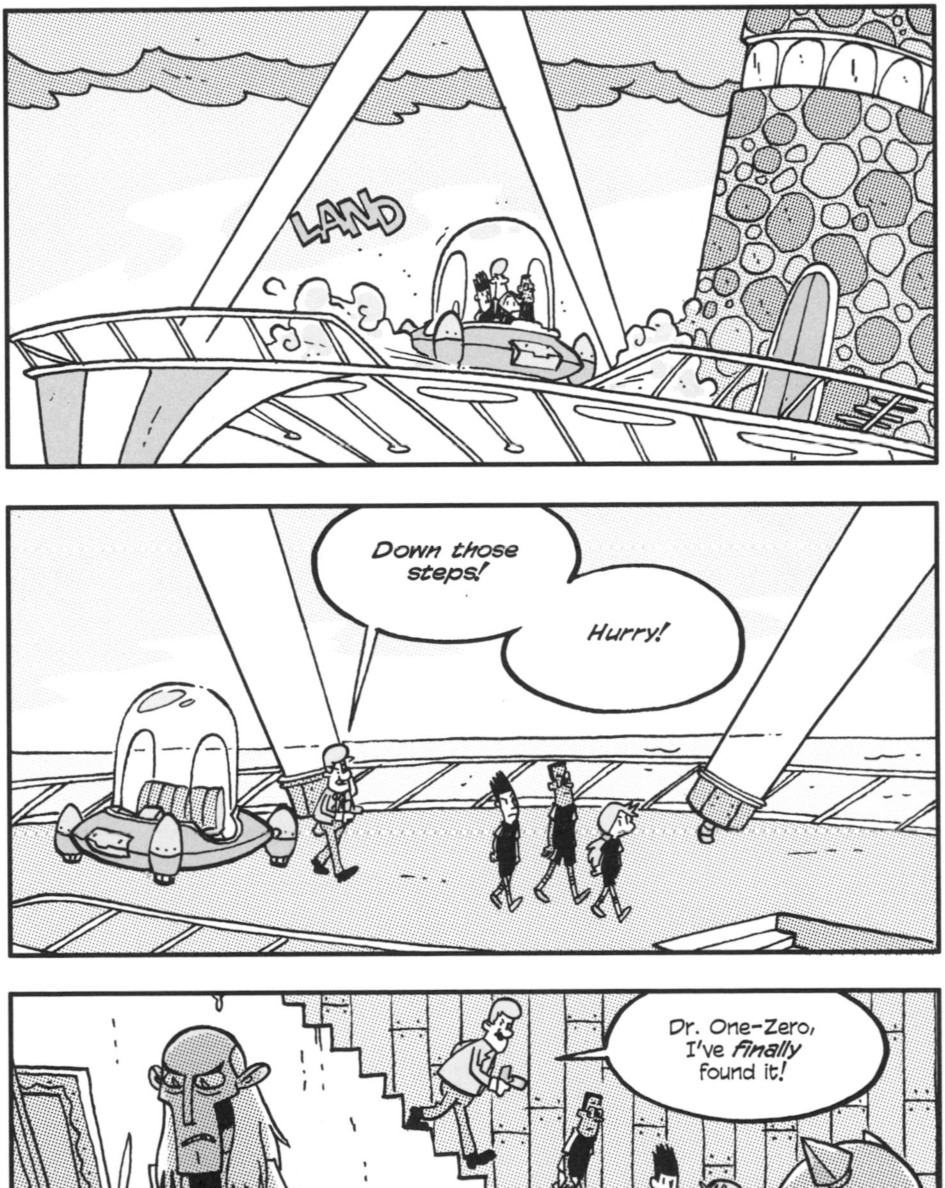
LAND
Down those steps!
Hurry!
Dr. One-Zero, I've *finally* found it!
Is that so, Principal Dean?

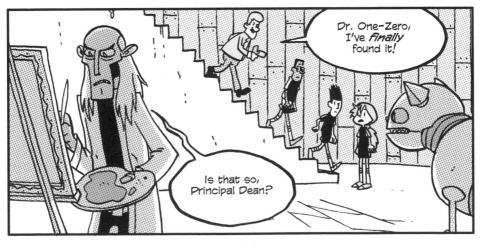

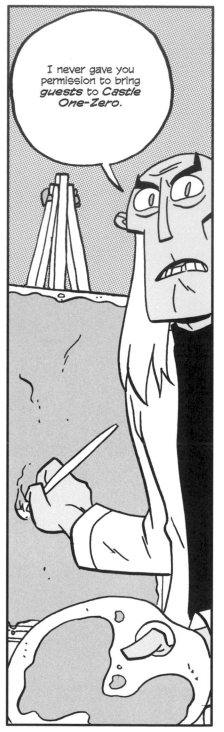

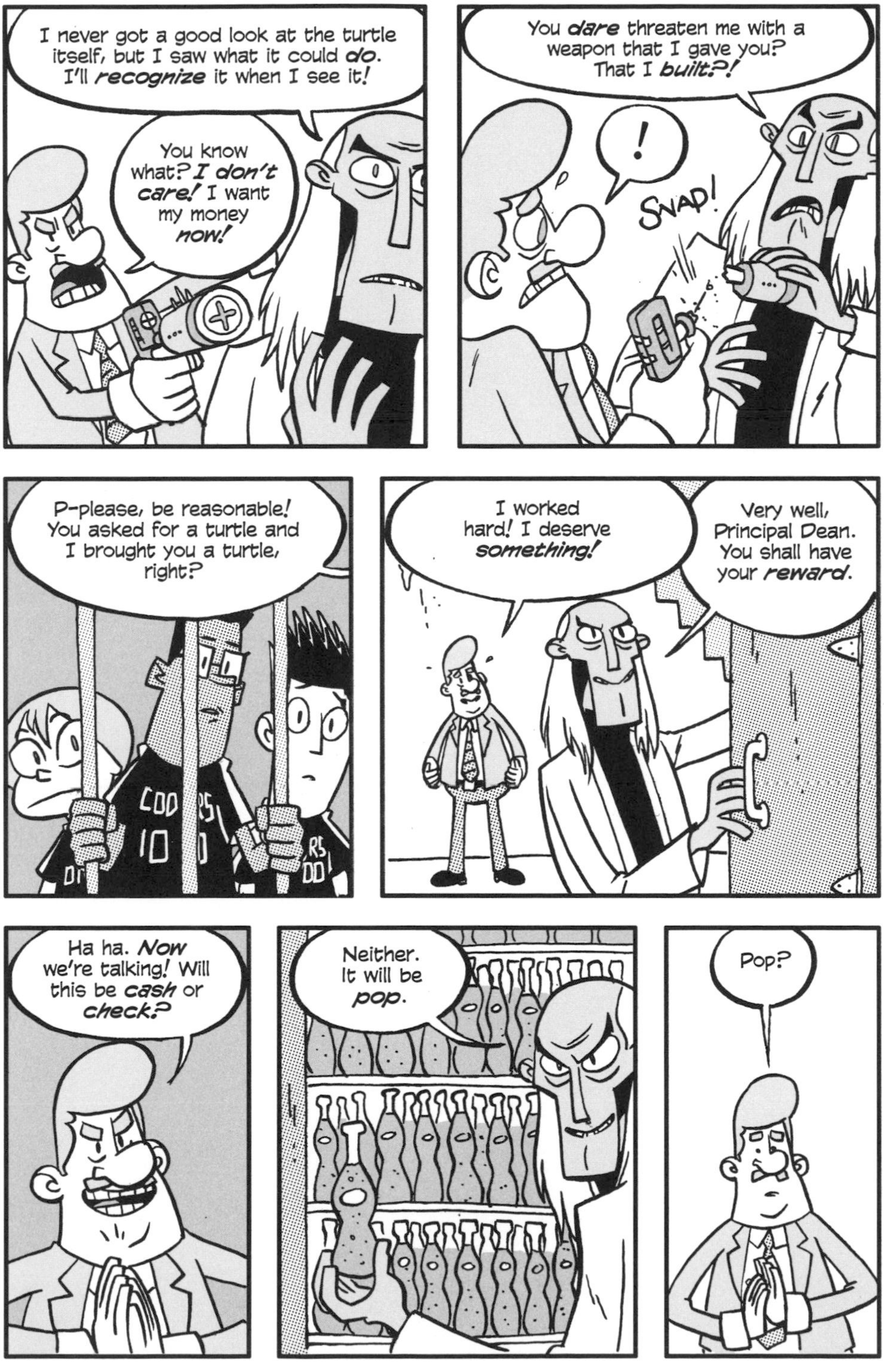
I never got a good look at the turtle itself, but I saw what it could *do*. I'll *recognize* it when I see it!
You know what? *I don't care!* I want my money *now!*
You *dare* threaten me with a weapon that I gave you? That I *built?!*
!
SNAP!
P-please, be reasonable! You asked for a turtle and I brought you a turtle, right?
I worked hard! I deserve *something!*
Very well, Principal Dean. You shall have your *reward*.
Ha ha. *Now* we're talking! Will this be *cash* or *check?*
Neither. It will be *pop*.
Pop?

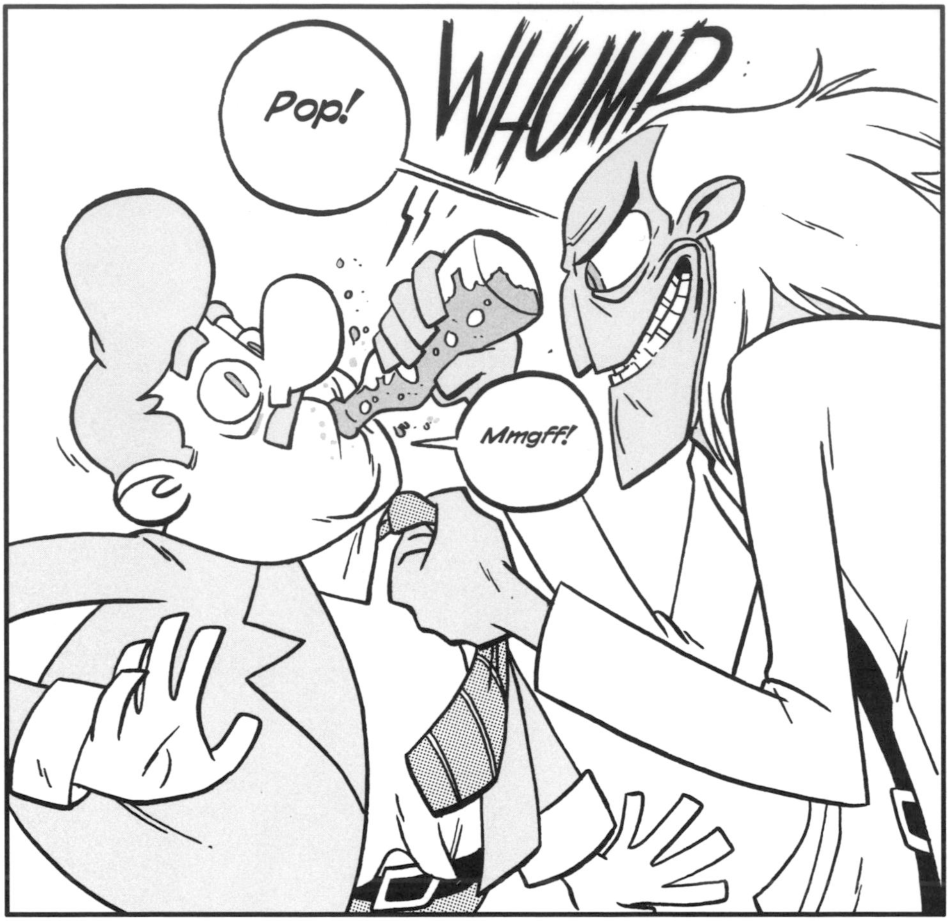
WHUMP
Pop!
Mmgff!

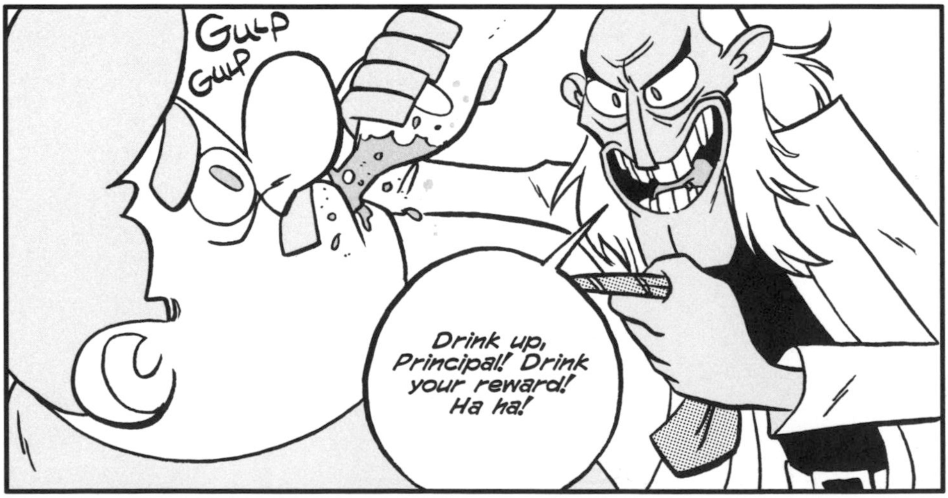
GULP
GULP
Drink up, Principal! Drink your reward! Ha ha!

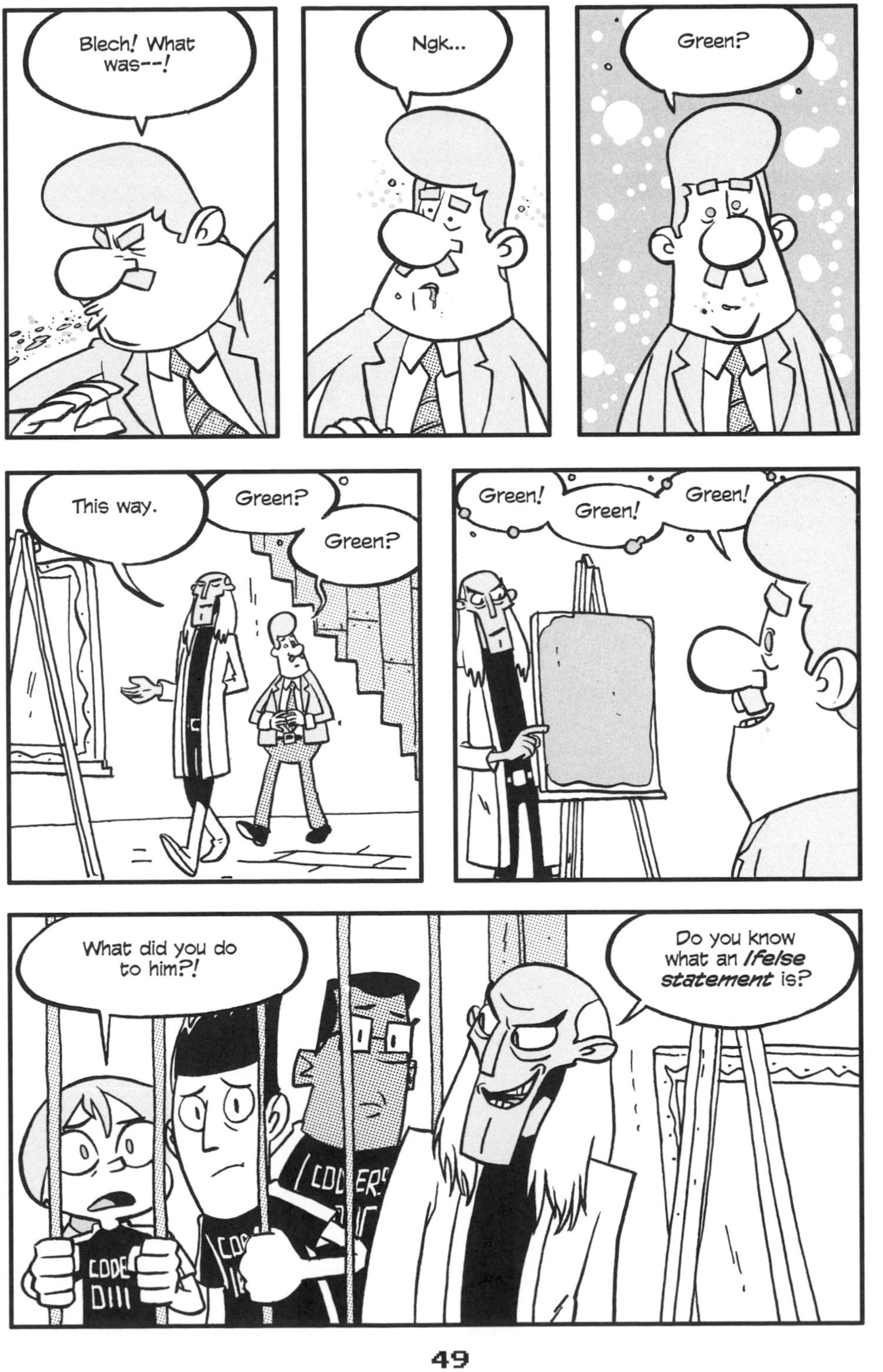
Blech! What was--!
Ngk...
Green?
This way.
Green?
Green?
Green!
Green!
Green!
What did you do to him?!
Do you know what an *If/else statement* is?

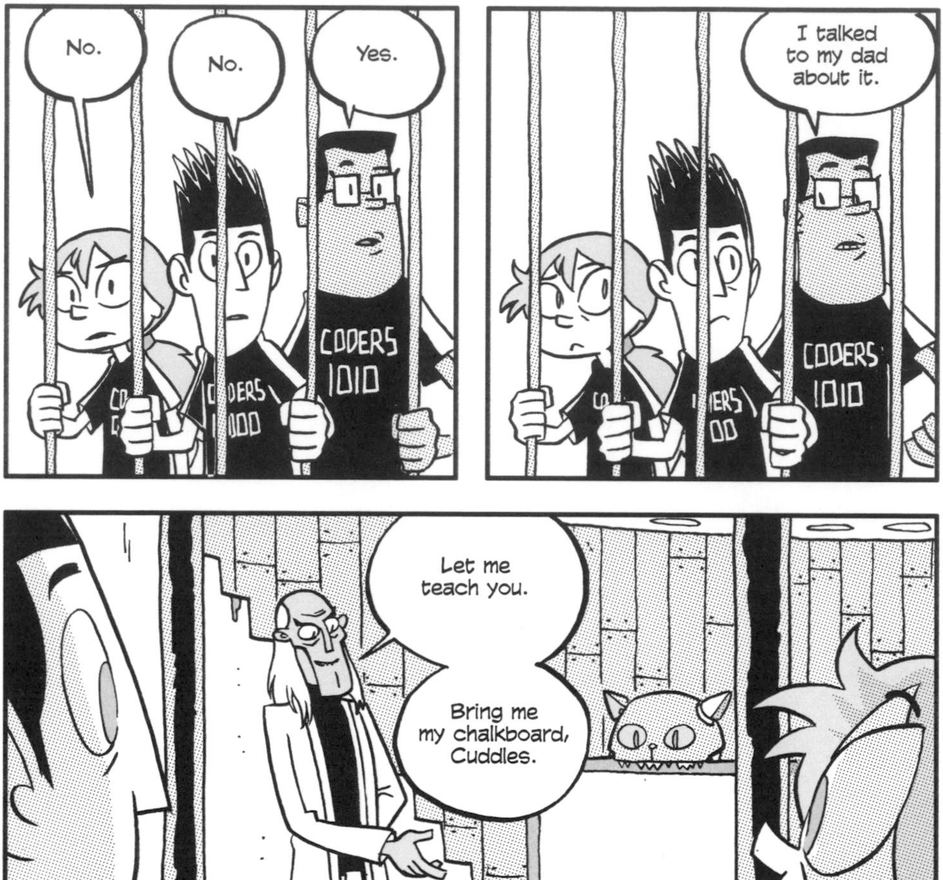
No.
No.
Yes.
CODERS 1010
I talked to my dad about it.
Let me teach you.
Bring me my chalkboard, Cuddles.
An Ifelse statement looks like this.
IFELSE( )[
][

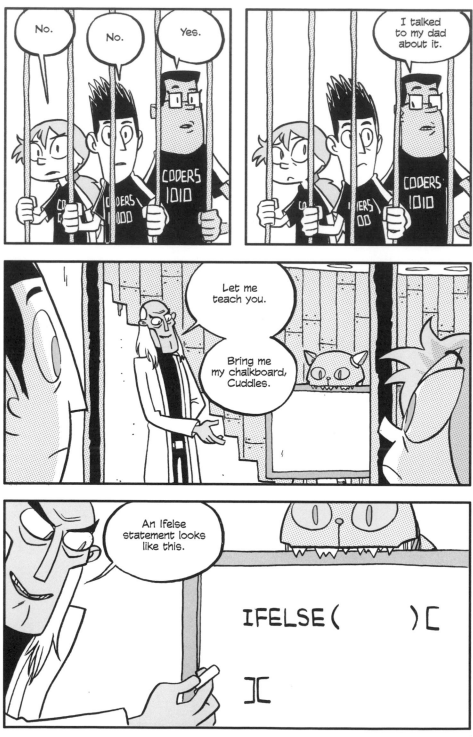

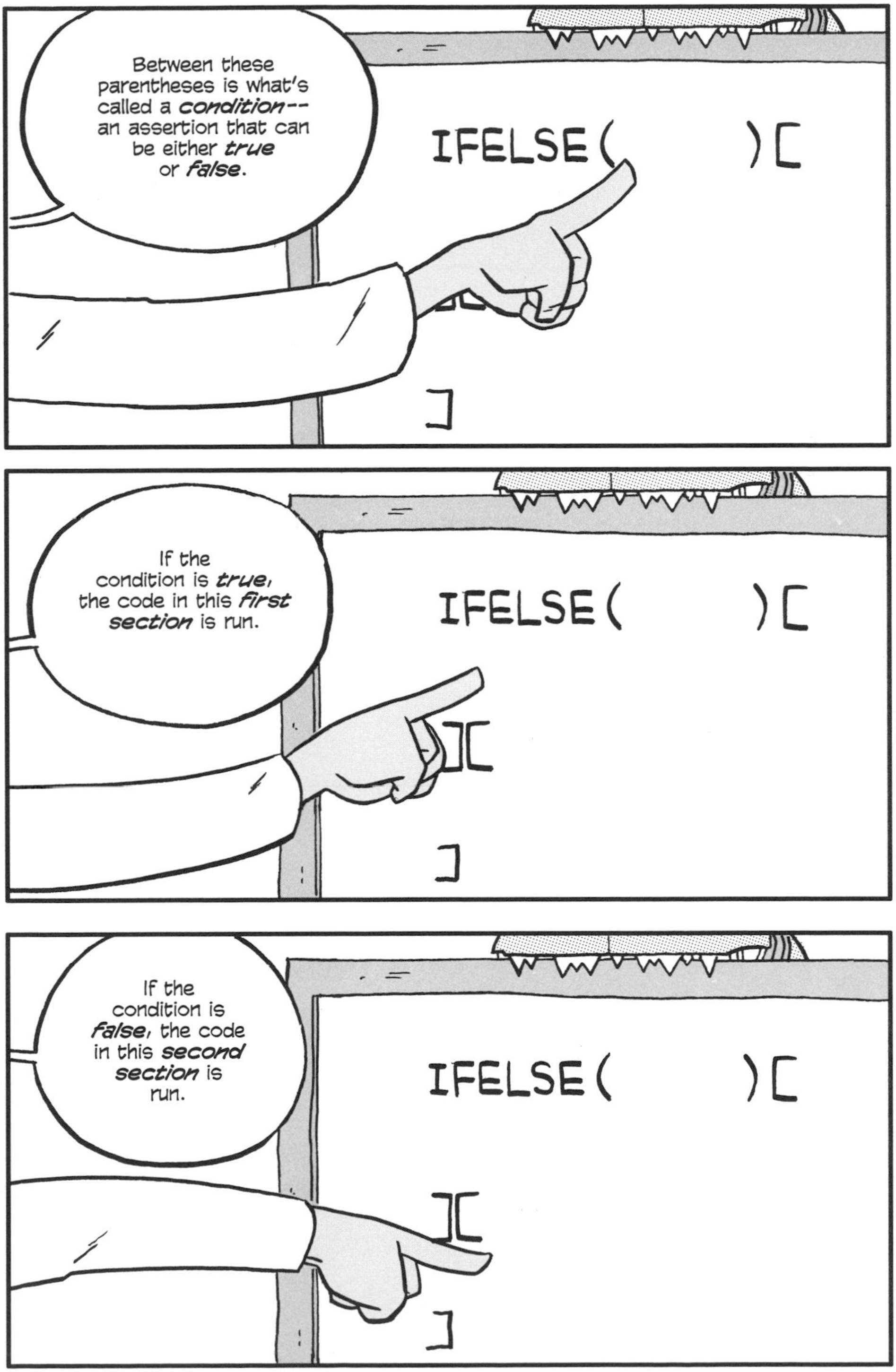
Between these parentheses is what's called a *condition*-- an assertion that can be either *true* or *false*.
IFELSE( )[
]
If the condition is *true*, the code in this *first section* is run.
IFELSE( )[
][
]
If the condition is *false*, the code in this *second section* is run.
IFELSE( )[
][
]

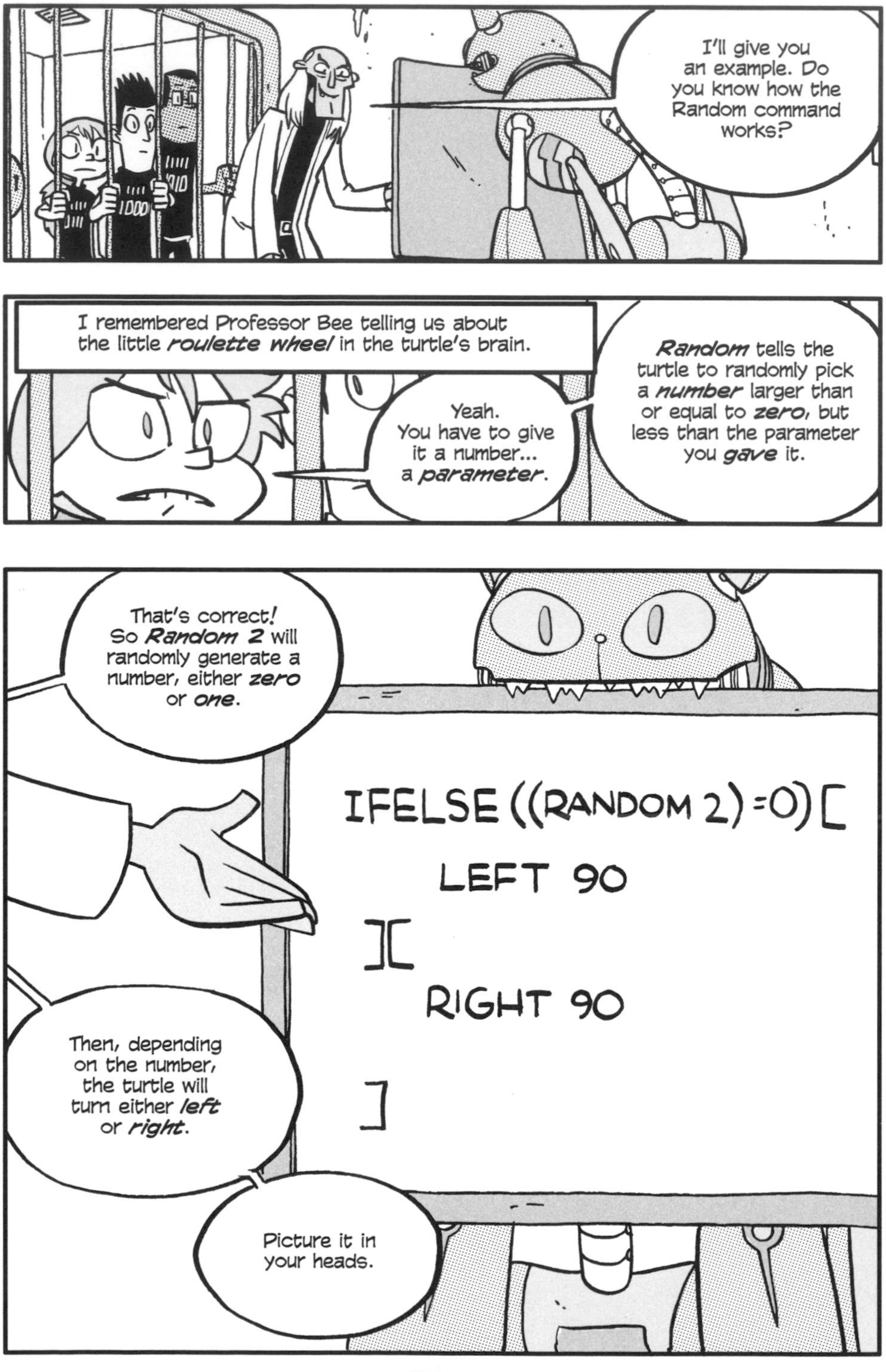
I'll give you an example. Do you know how the Random command works?
I remembered Professor Bee telling us about the little *roulette wheel* in the turtle's brain.
Yeah. You have to give it a number... a *parameter*.
Random tells the turtle to randomly pick a *number* larger than or equal to *zero*, but less than the parameter you *gave* it.
That's correct! So *Random 2* will randomly generate a number, either *zero* or *one*.
IFELSE ((RANDOM 2) =0) [
LEFT 90
] [
RIGHT 90
]
Then, depending on the number, the turtle will turn either *left* or *right*.
Picture it in your heads.

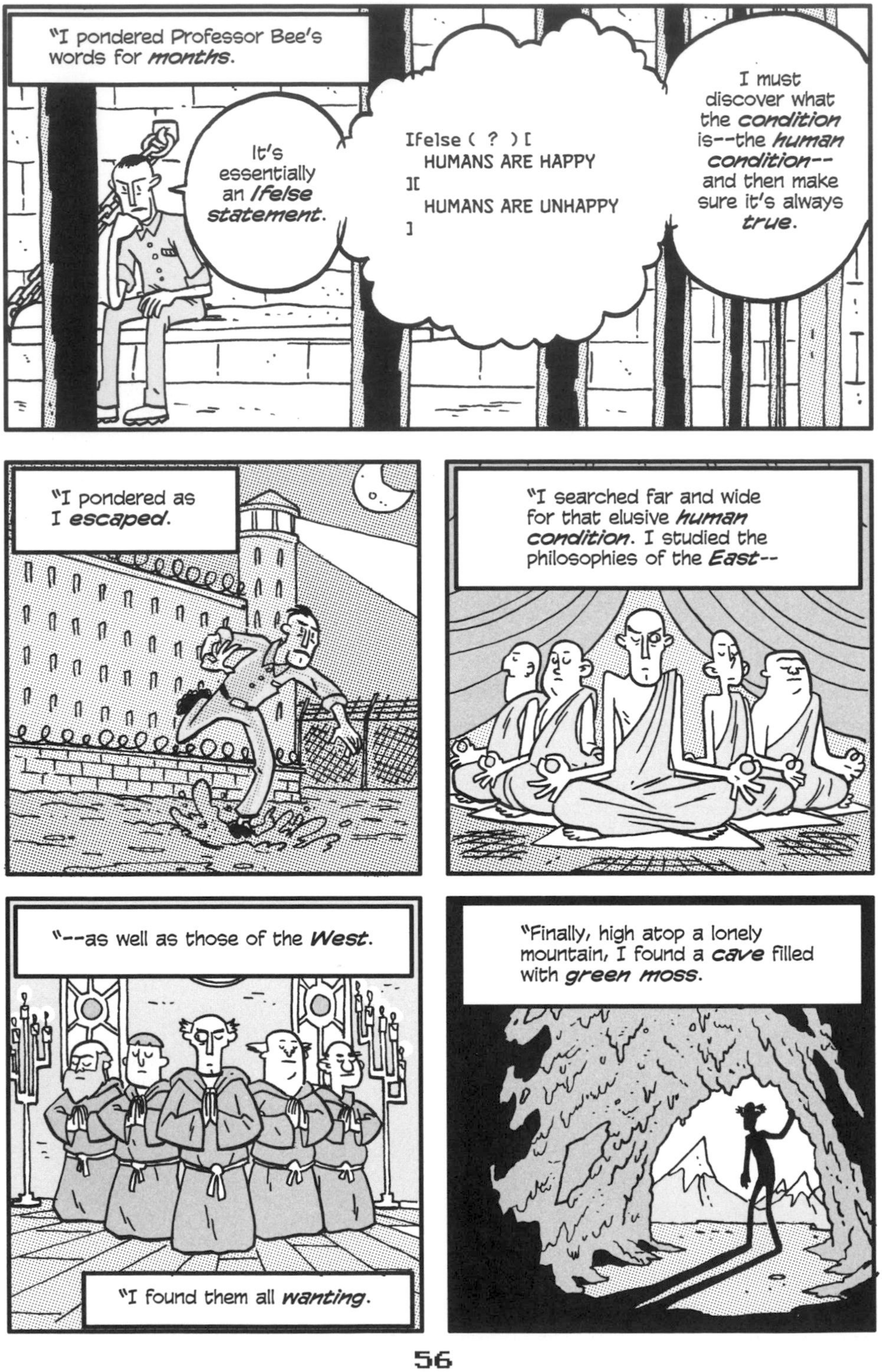
"I pondered Professor Bee's words for *months*.
It's essentially an *Ifelse statement*.
Ifelse (?) [
HUMANS ARE HAPPY
][
HUMANS ARE UNHAPPY
]
I must discover what the *condition* is--the *human condition*-- and then make sure it's always *true*.
"I pondered as I *escaped*.
"I searched far and wide for that elusive *human condition*. I studied the philosophies of the *East*--
"--as well as those of the *West*.
"I found them all *wanting*.
"Finally, high atop a lonely mountain, I found a *cave* filled with *green moss*.

59

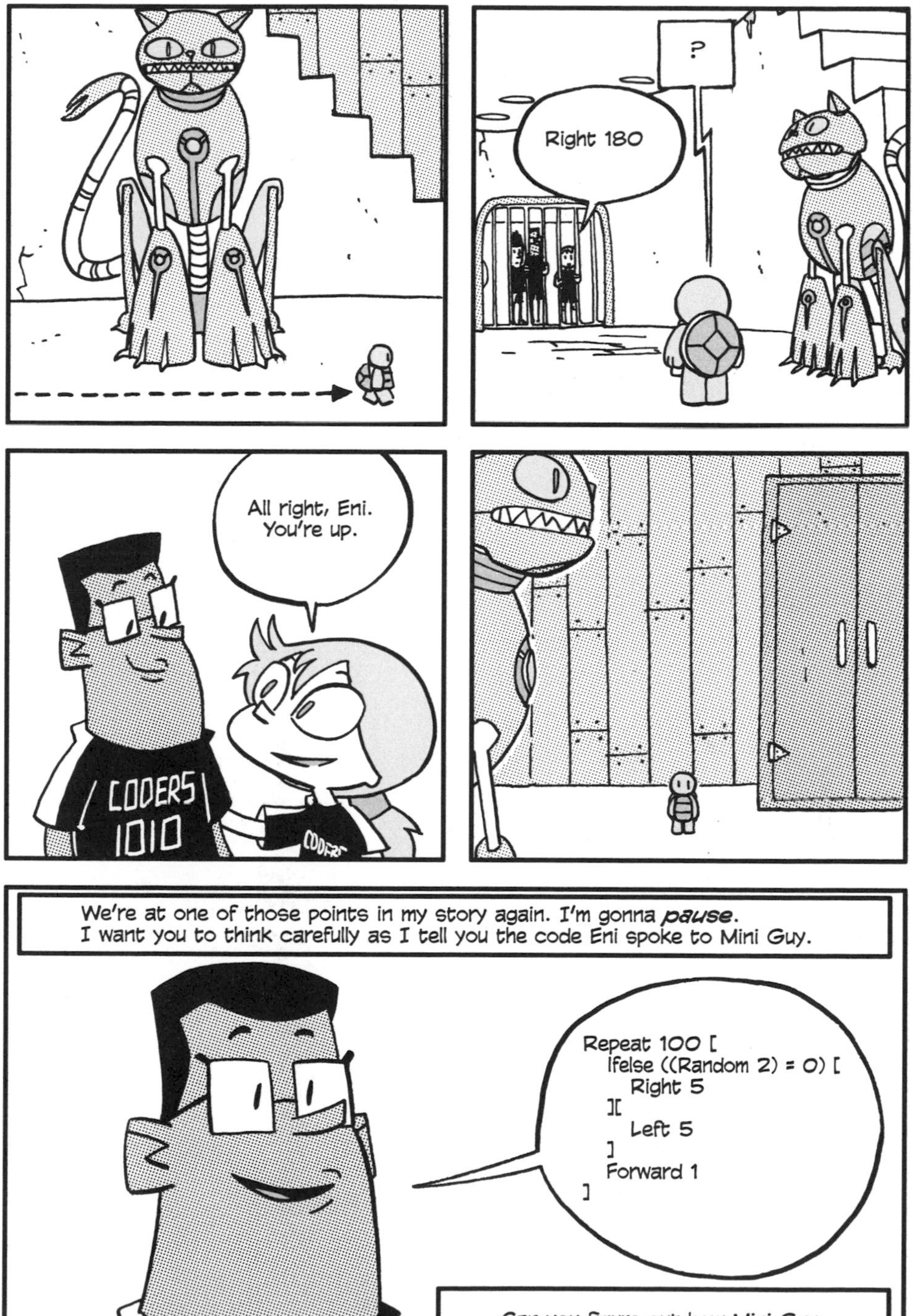
Right 180
?
All right, Eni. You're up.
CODERS 1010
We're at one of those points in my story again. I'm gonna *pause*.
I want you to think carefully as I tell you the code Eni spoke to Mini Guy.
Repeat 100 [
   Ifelse ((Random 2) = 0) [
      Right 5
   ][
      Left 5
   ]
   Forward 1
]
Can you figure out how Mini Guy is going to move?

Chapter

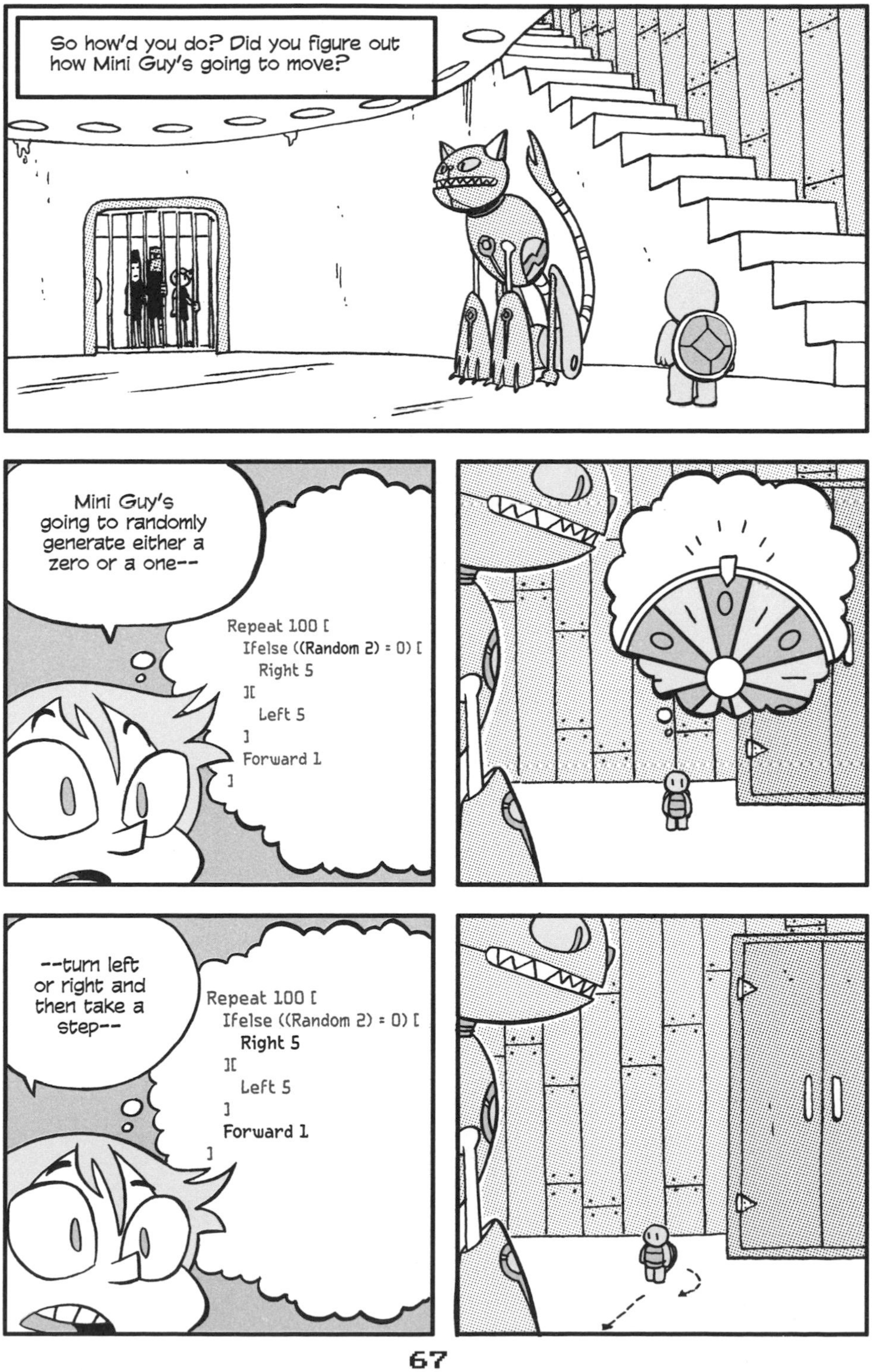

So how'd you do? Did you figure out how Mini Guy's going to move?
Mini Guy's going to randomly generate either a zero or a one--
Repeat 100 [
Ifelse ((Random 2) = 0) [
Right 5
][
Left 5
]
Forward 1
]
--turn left or right and then take a step--
Repeat 100 [
Ifelse ((Random 2) = 0) [
Right 5
][
Left 5
]
Forward 1
]

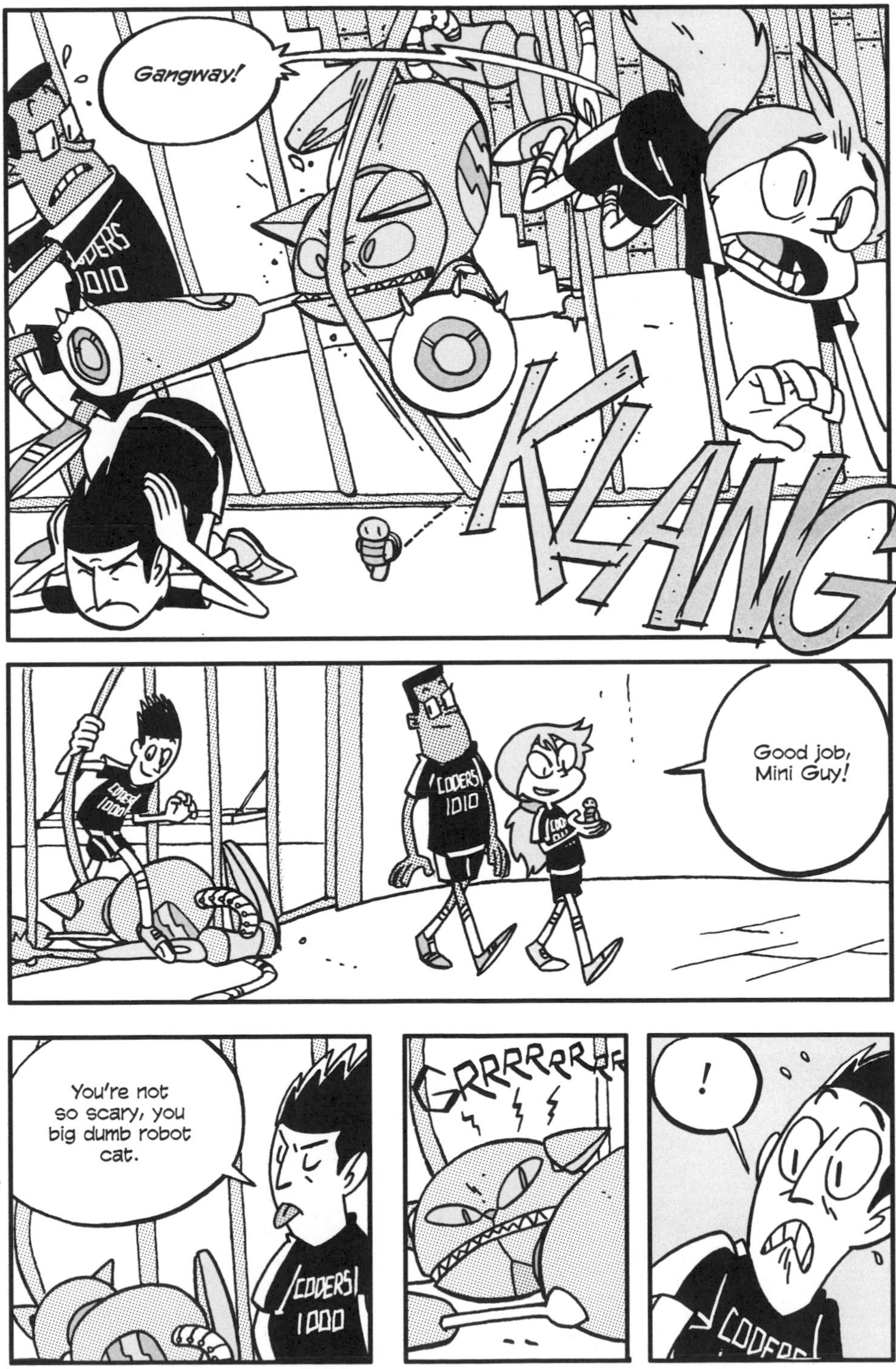
Gangway!
KLANG
Good job, Mini Guy!
You're not so scary, you big dumb robot cat.
GRRRRRRRR
!

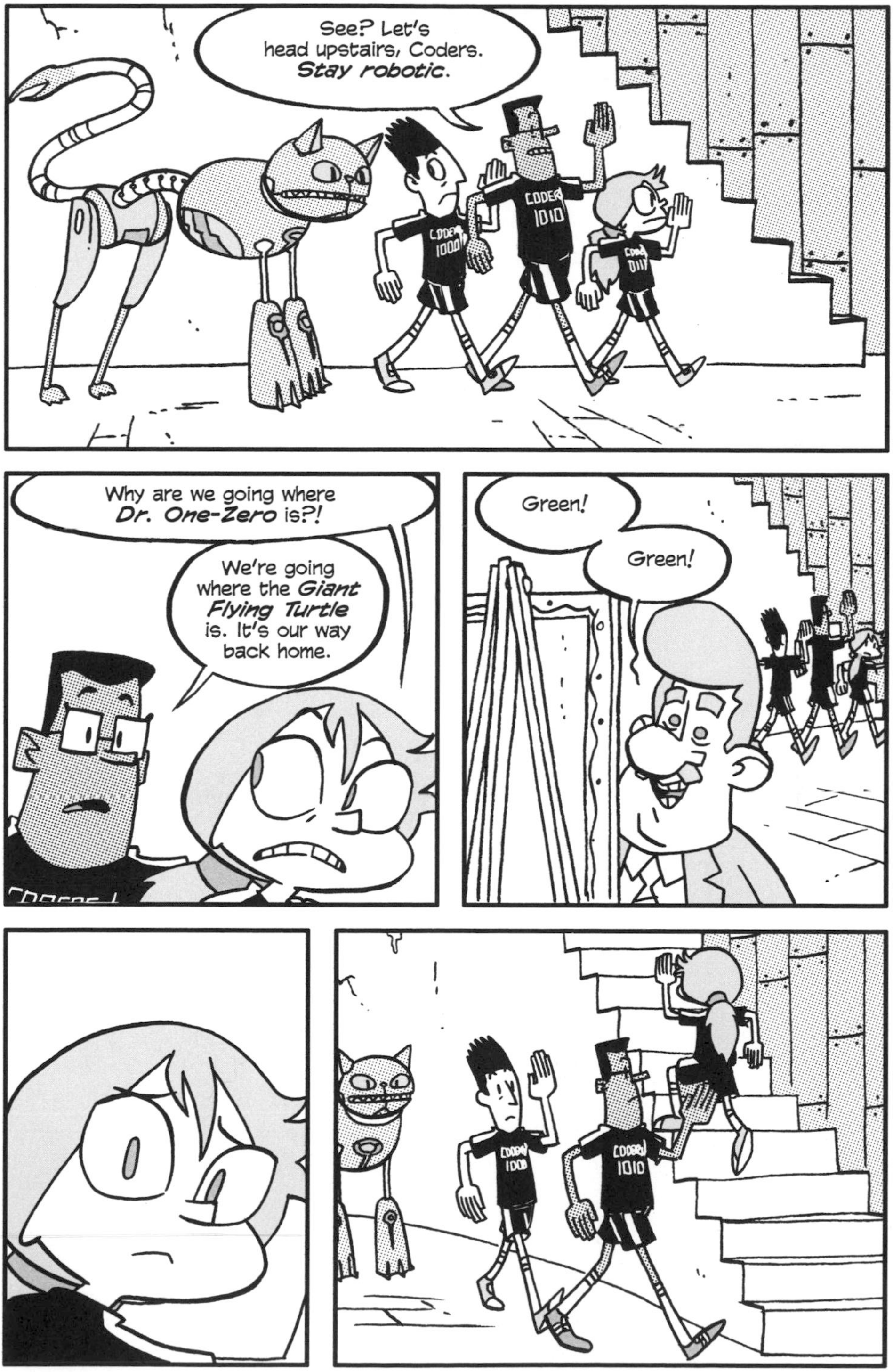

See? Let's head upstairs, Coders. *Stay robotic*.
CODER 1000
CODER 1010
Why are we going where *Dr. One-Zero* is?!
We're going where the *Giant Flying Turtle* is. It's our way back home.
Green!
Green!
CODER 1000
CODER 1010

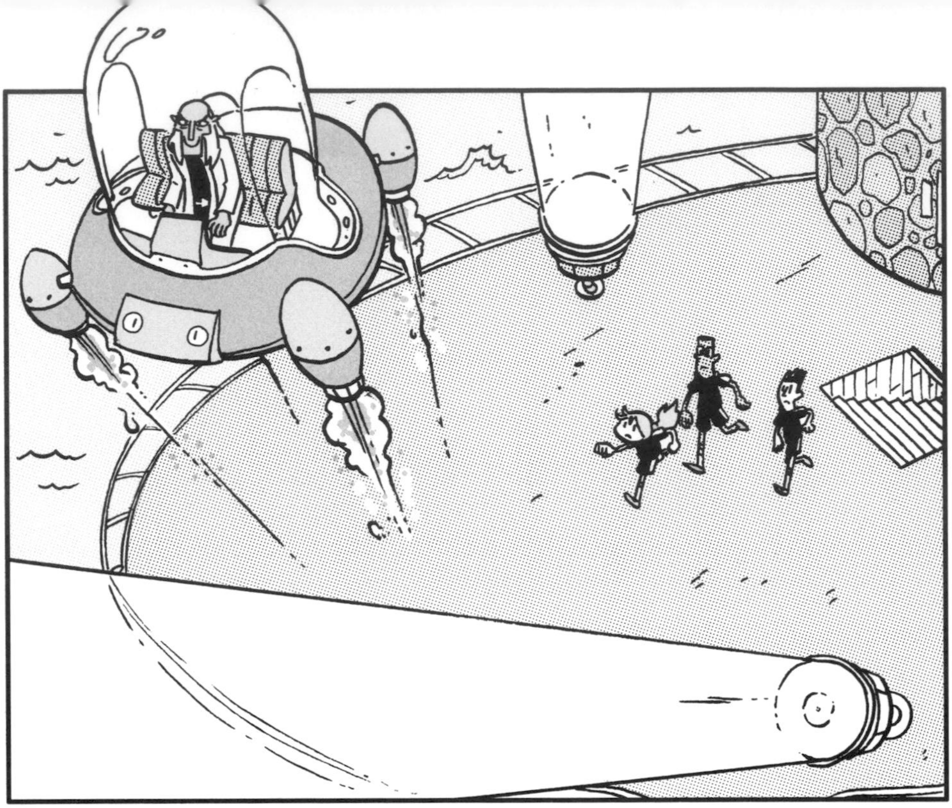

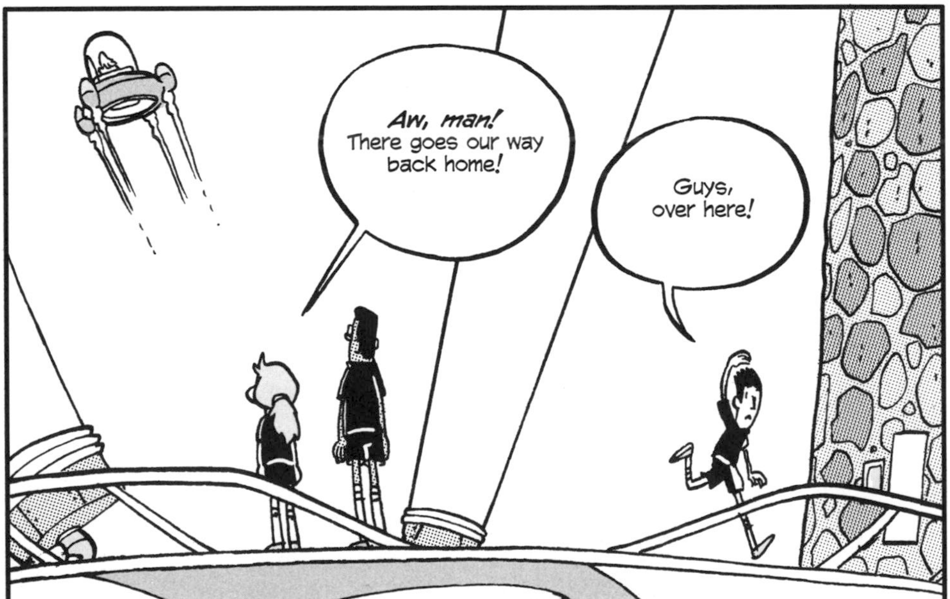
Aw, man! There goes our way back home!
Guys, over here!

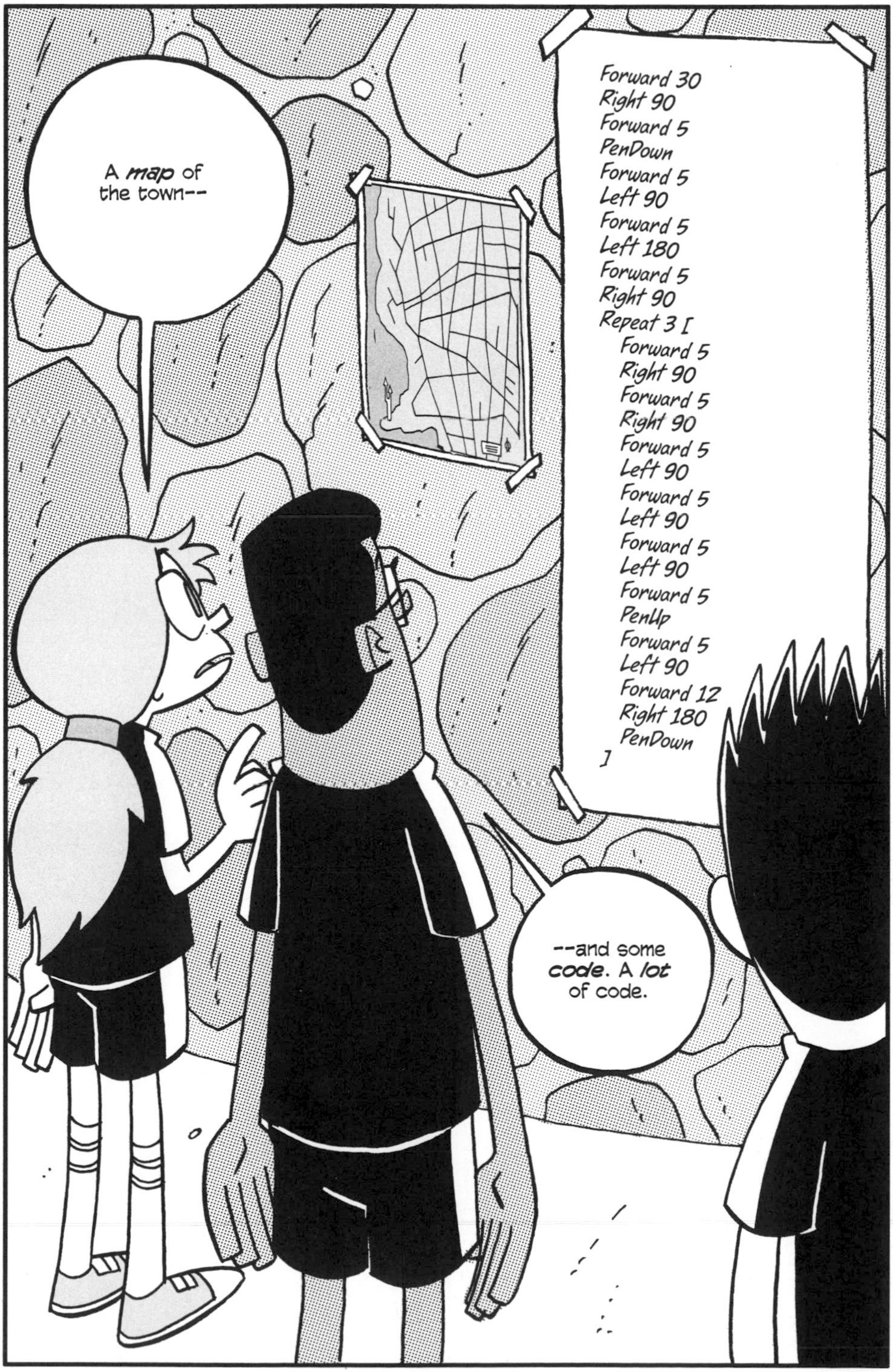
A map of the town--
Forward 30
Right 90
Forward 5
PenDown
Forward 5
Left 90
Forward 5
Left 180
Forward 5
Right 90
Repeat 3 [
Forward 5
Right 90
Forward 5
Right 90
Forward 5
Left 90
Forward 5
Left 90
Forward 5
Left 90
Forward 5
PenUp
Forward 5
Left 90
Forward 12
Right 180
PenDown
]
--and some code. A lot of code.

79

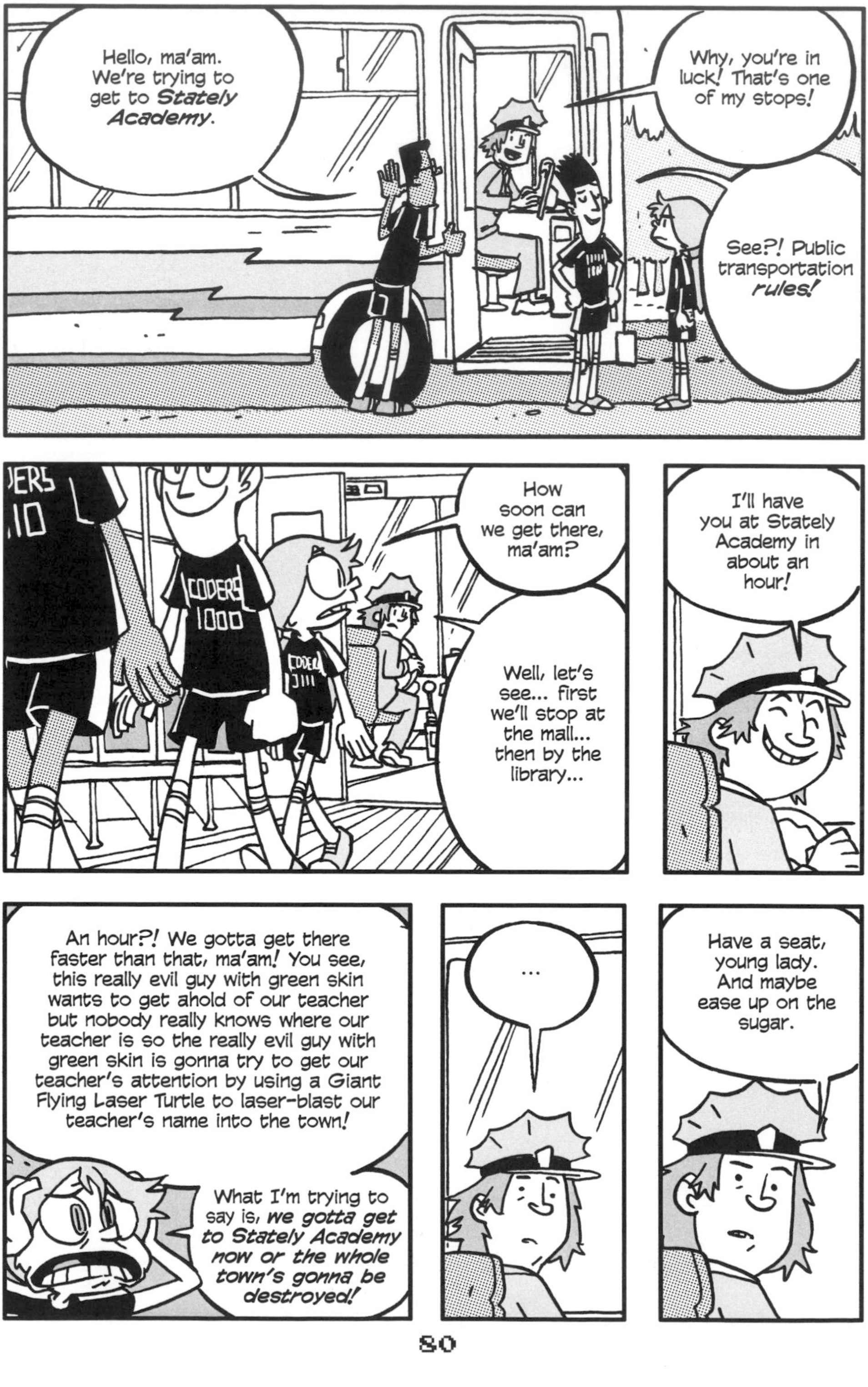
Hello, ma'am. We're trying to get to *Stately Academy*.
Why, you're in luck! That's one of my stops!
See?! Public transportation *rules!*
How soon can we get there, ma'am?
Well, let's see... first we'll stop at the mall... then by the library...
I'll have you at Stately Academy in about an hour!
An hour?! We gotta get there faster than that, ma'am! You see, this really evil guy with green skin wants to get ahold of our teacher but nobody really knows where our teacher is so the really evil guy with green skin is gonna try to get our teacher's attention by using a Giant Flying Laser Turtle to laser-blast our teacher's name into the town!
What I'm trying to say is, ***we gotta get to Stately Academy now or the whole town's gonna be destroyed!***
...
Have a seat, young lady. And maybe ease up on the sugar.

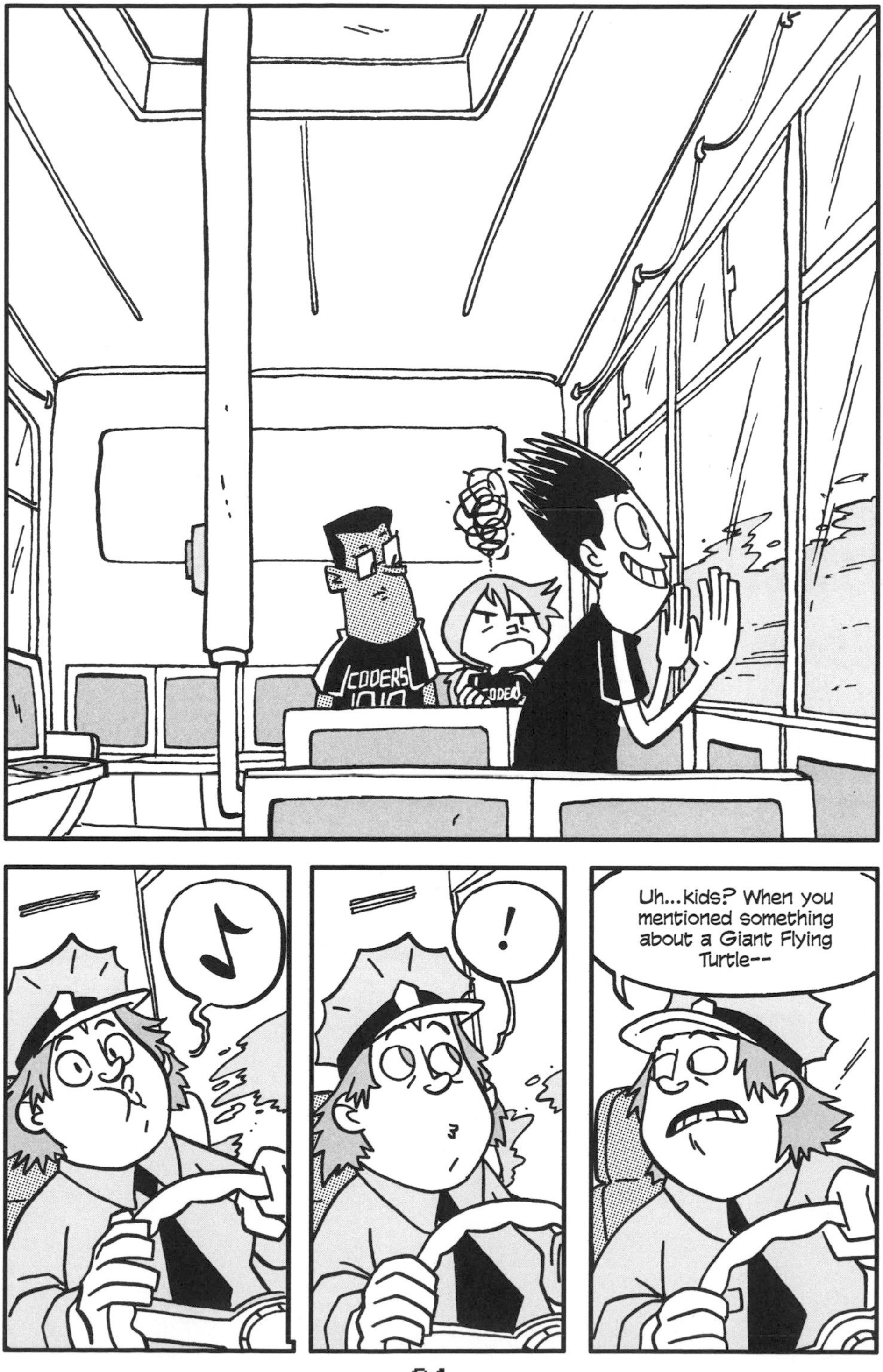
CODERS
CODERS
!
Uh...kids? When you mentioned something about a Giant Flying Turtle--

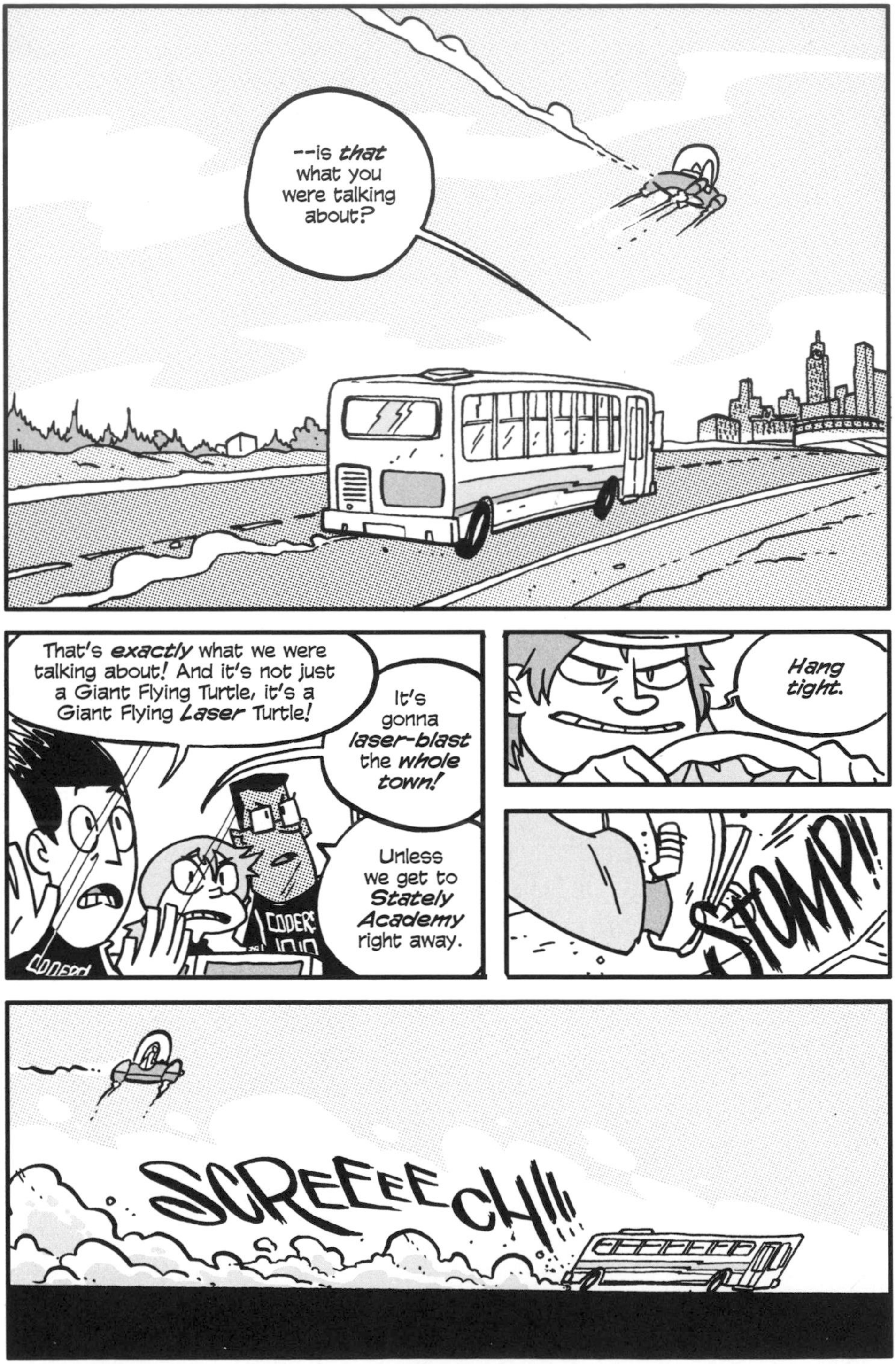

--is *that* what you were talking about?
That's *exactly* what we were talking about! And it's not just a Giant Flying Turtle, it's a Giant Flying *Laser* Turtle!
It's gonna *laser-blast* the *whole town!*
Unless we get to *Stately Academy* right away.
Hang tight.
STOMP!!
SCREEEECH!!!

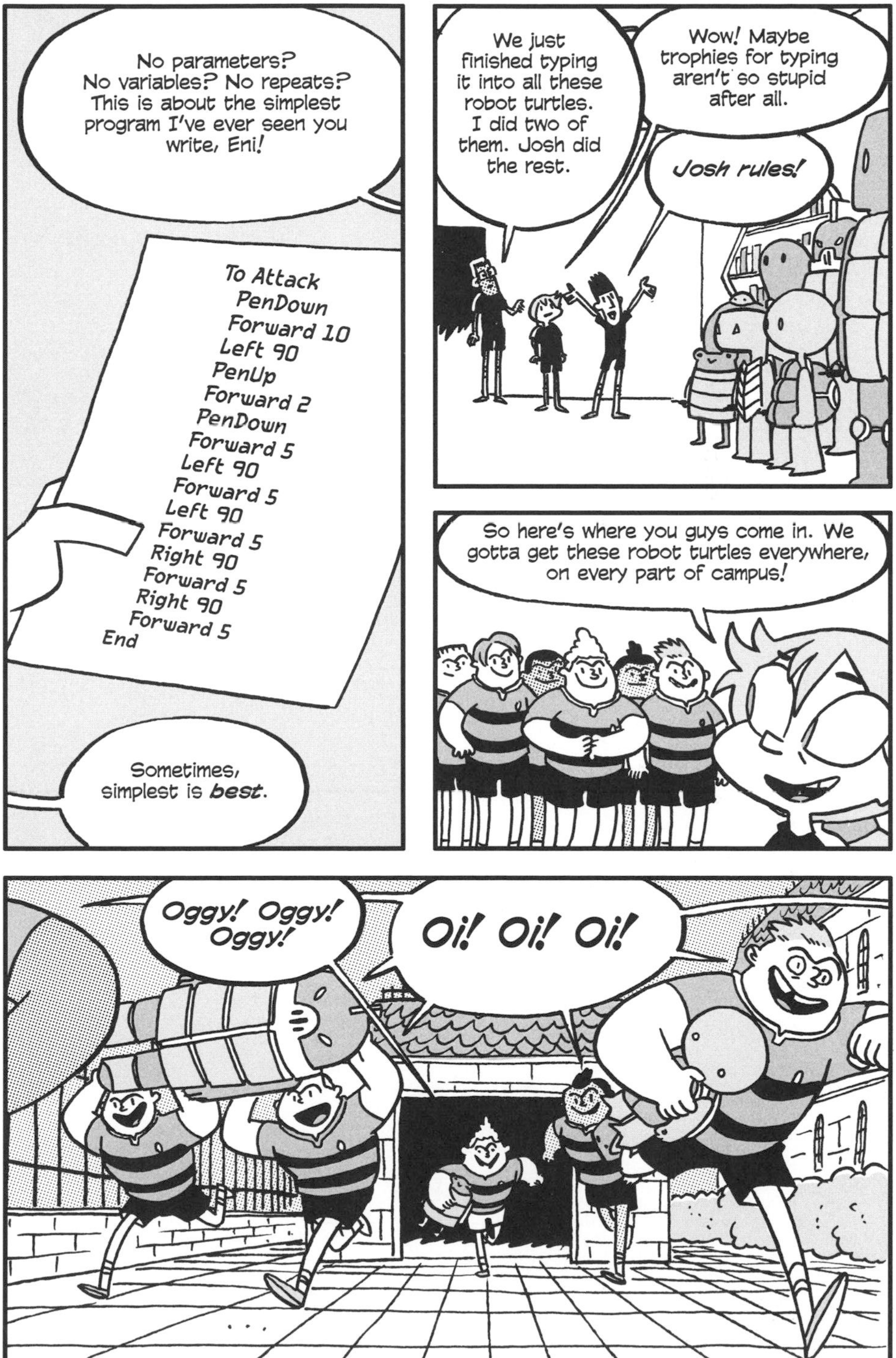
No parameters? No variables? No repeats? This is about the simplest program I've ever seen you write, Eni!
To Attack
PenDown
Forward 10
Left 90
PenUp
Forward 2
PenDown
Forward 5
Left 90
Forward 5
Left 90
Forward 5
Right 90
Forward 5
Right 90
Forward 5
End
Sometimes, simplest is *best*.
We just finished typing it into all these robot turtles. I did two of them. Josh did the rest.
Wow! Maybe trophies for typing aren't so stupid after all.
Josh rules!
So here's where you guys come in. We gotta get these robot turtles everywhere, on every part of campus!
Oggy! Oggy! Oggy!
Oi! Oi! Oi!
. . .

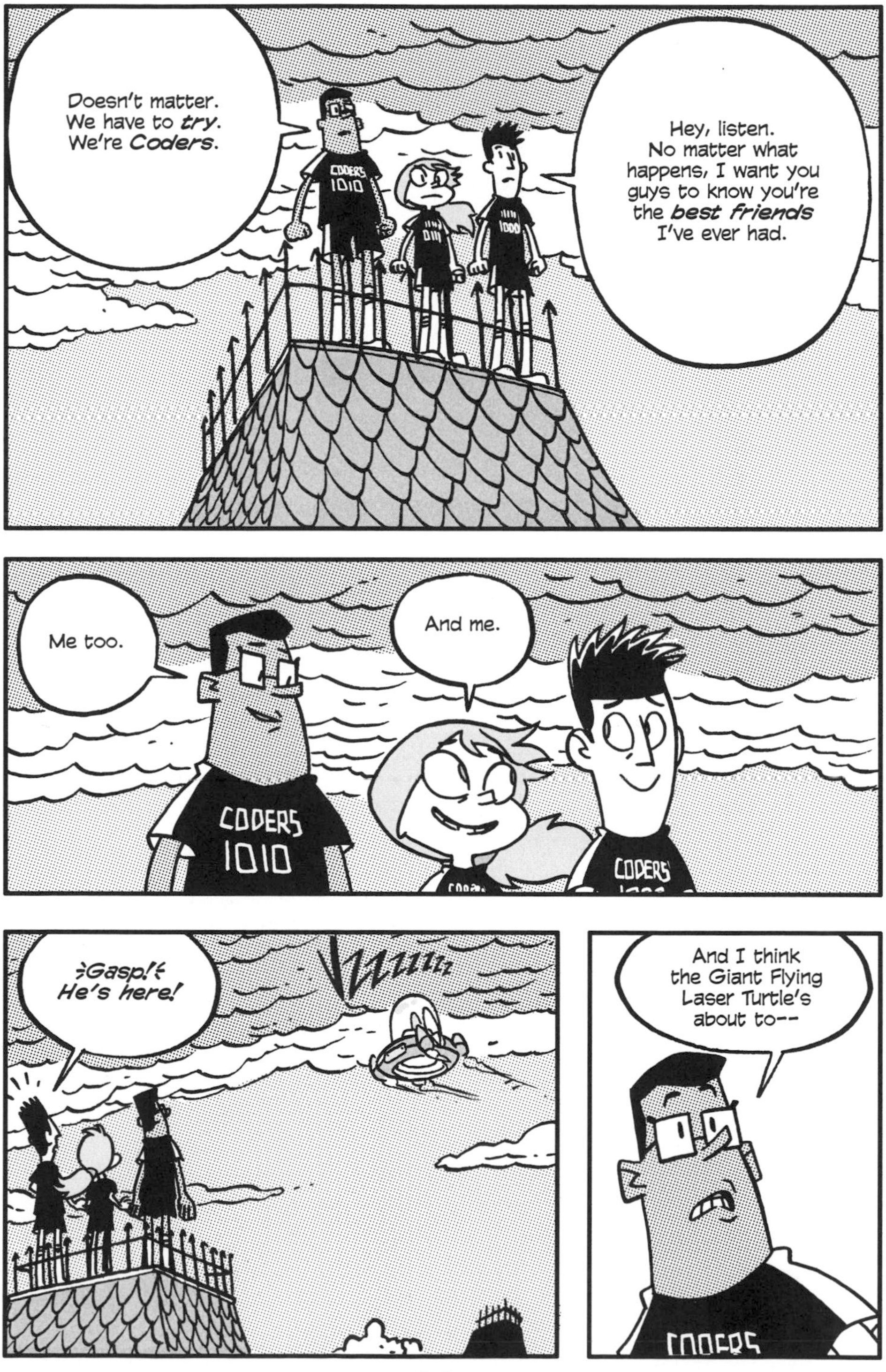

Doesn't matter. We have to *try*. We're *Coders*.
CODERS 1010
Hey, listen. No matter what happens, I want you guys to know you're the *best friends* I've ever had.
Me too.
And me.
CODERS 1010
CODERS
Gasp! He's here!
ZZZZZZZ
And I think the Giant Flying Laser Turtle's about to--

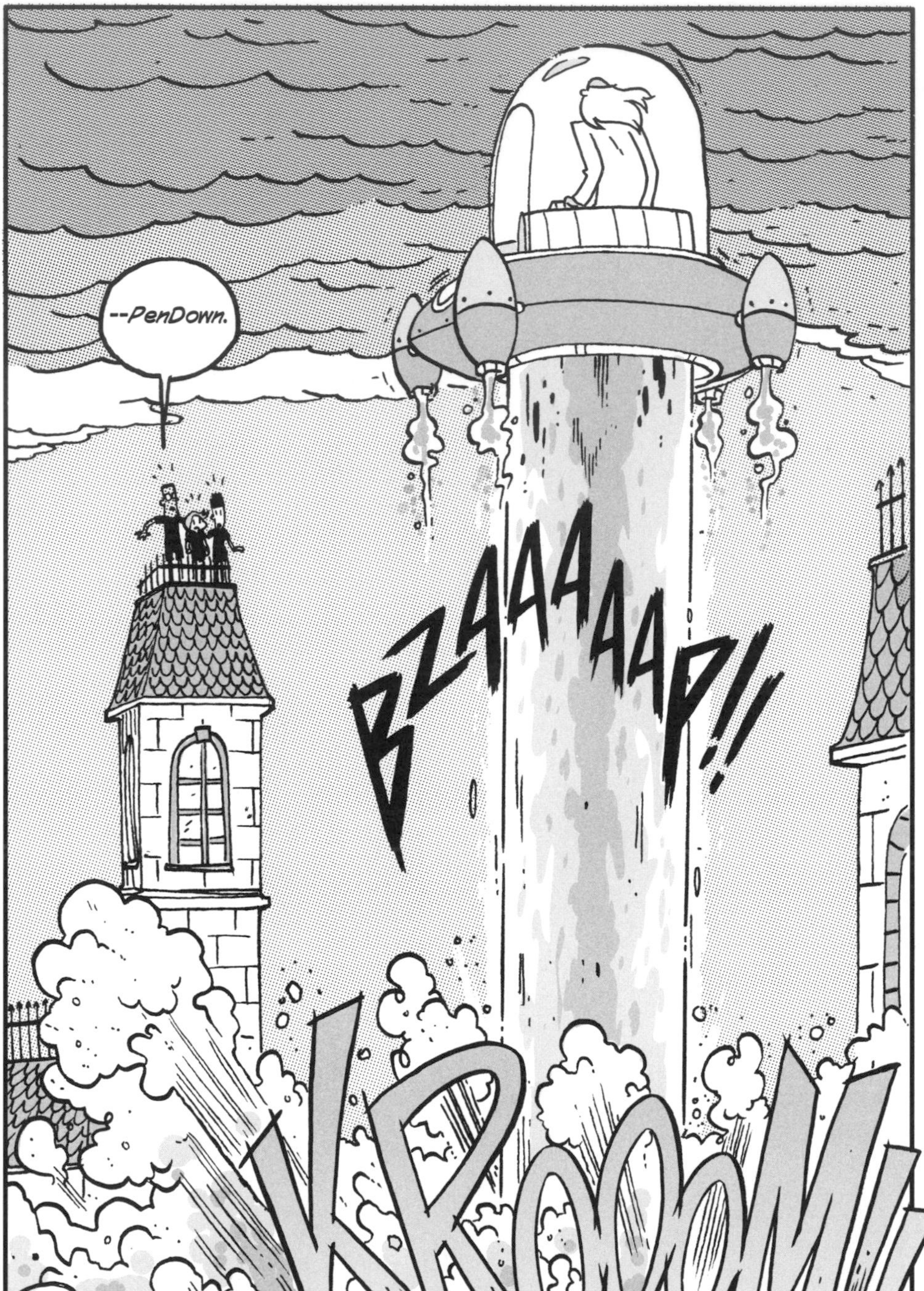
--PenDown.
BZAAAAAAP!!
KROOOM!!

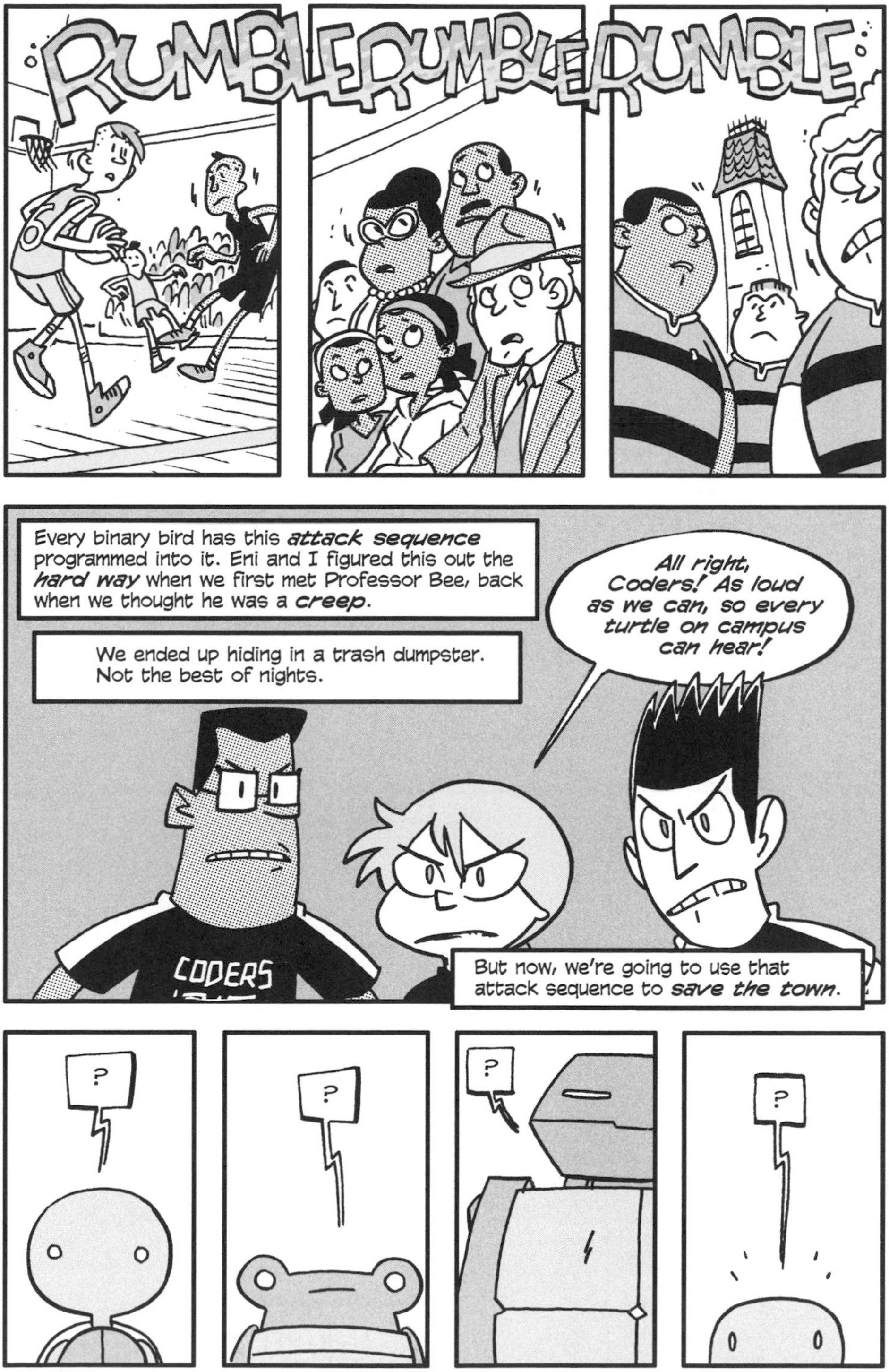
RUMBLE RUMBLE RUMBLE
Every binary bird has this *attack sequence* programmed into it. Eni and I figured this out the *hard way* when we first met Professor Bee, back when we thought he was a *creep*.
We ended up hiding in a trash dumpster. Not the best of nights.
All right, Coders! As loud as we can, so every turtle on campus can hear!
CODERS
But now, we're going to use that attack sequence to *save the town*.
?
?
?
?

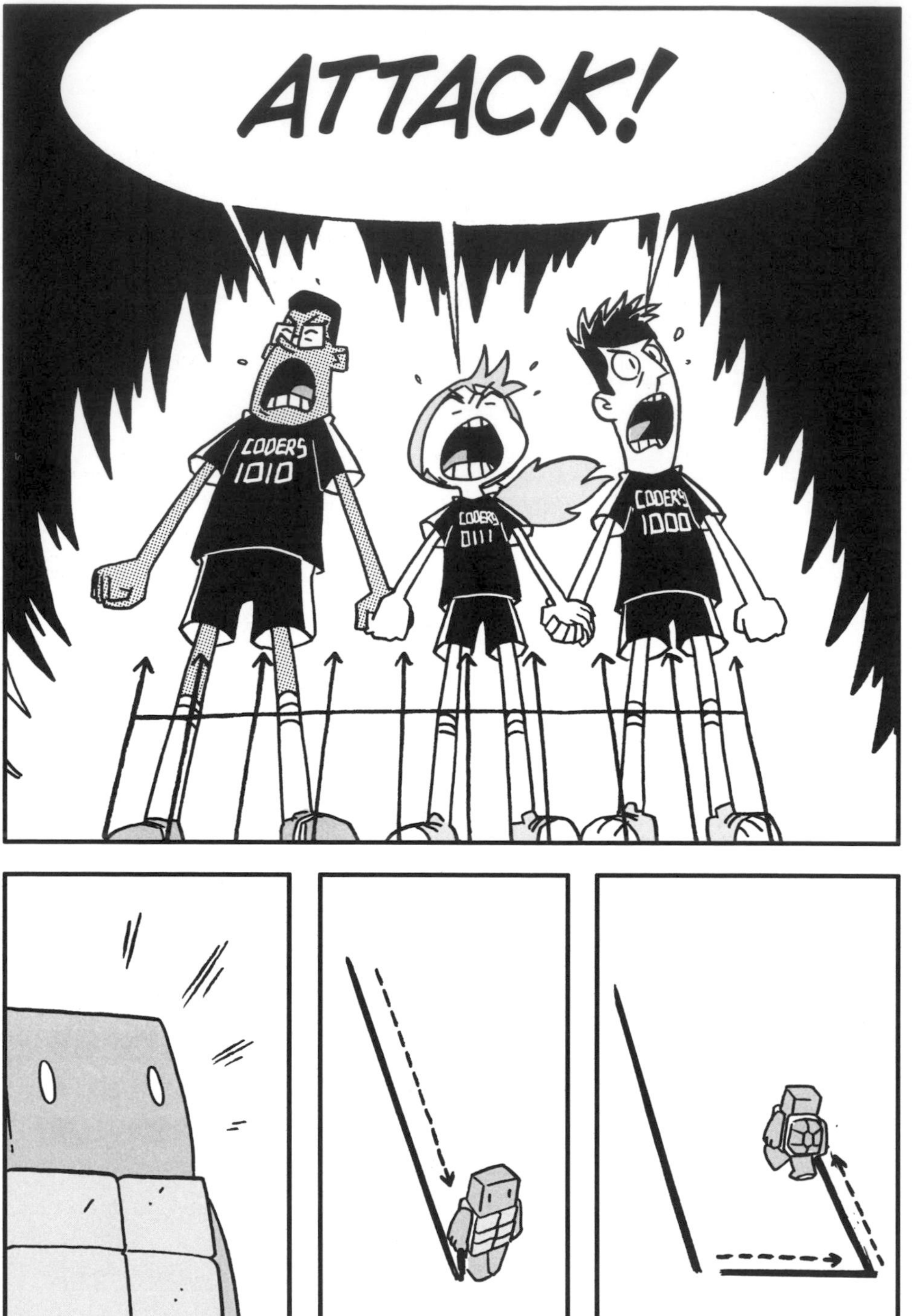
ATTACK!
CODERS 1010
CODERS 0111
CODERS 1000

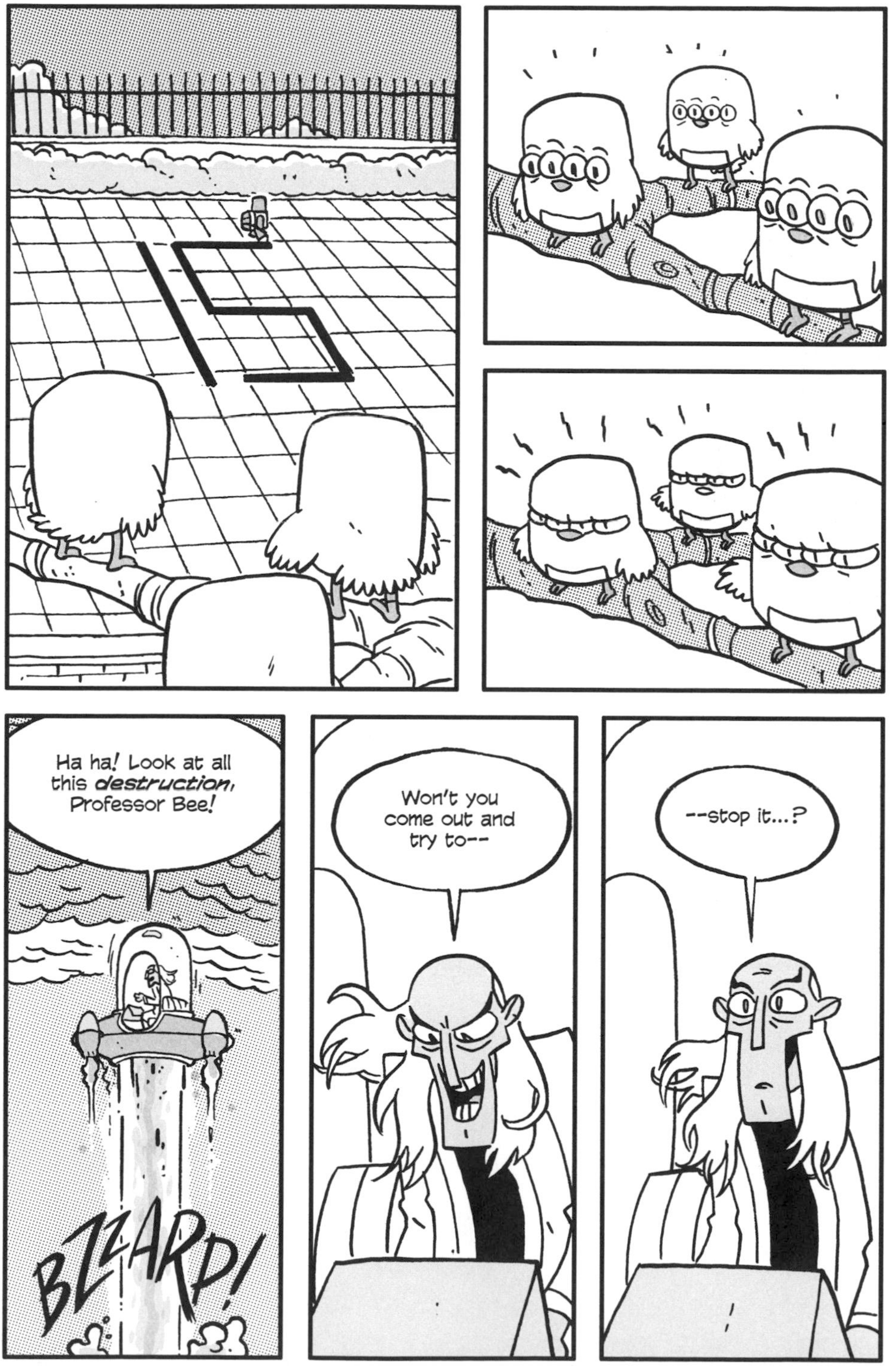
Ha ha! Look at all this *destruction*, Professor Bee!
BZZARD!
Won't you come out and try to--
--stop it...?

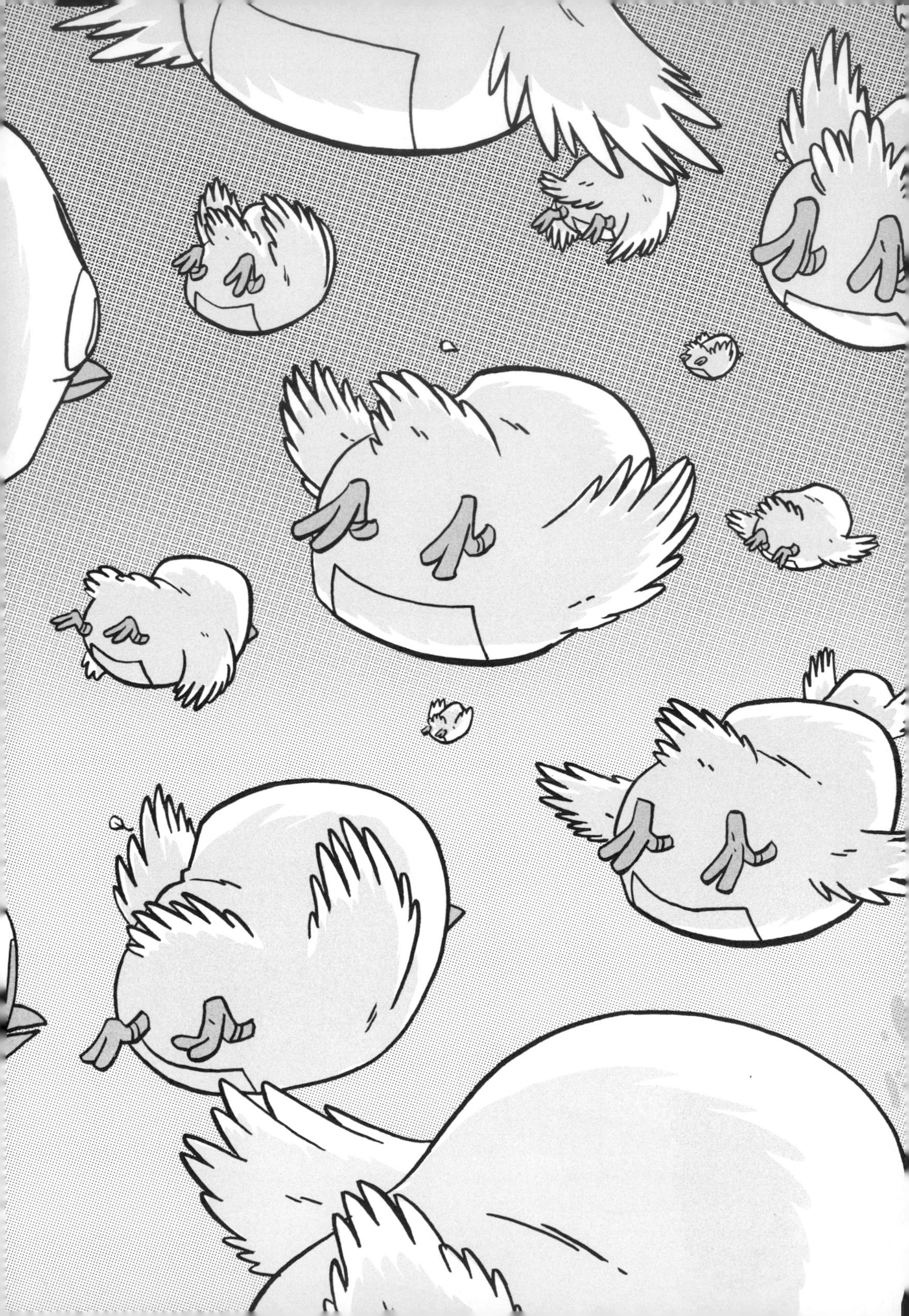

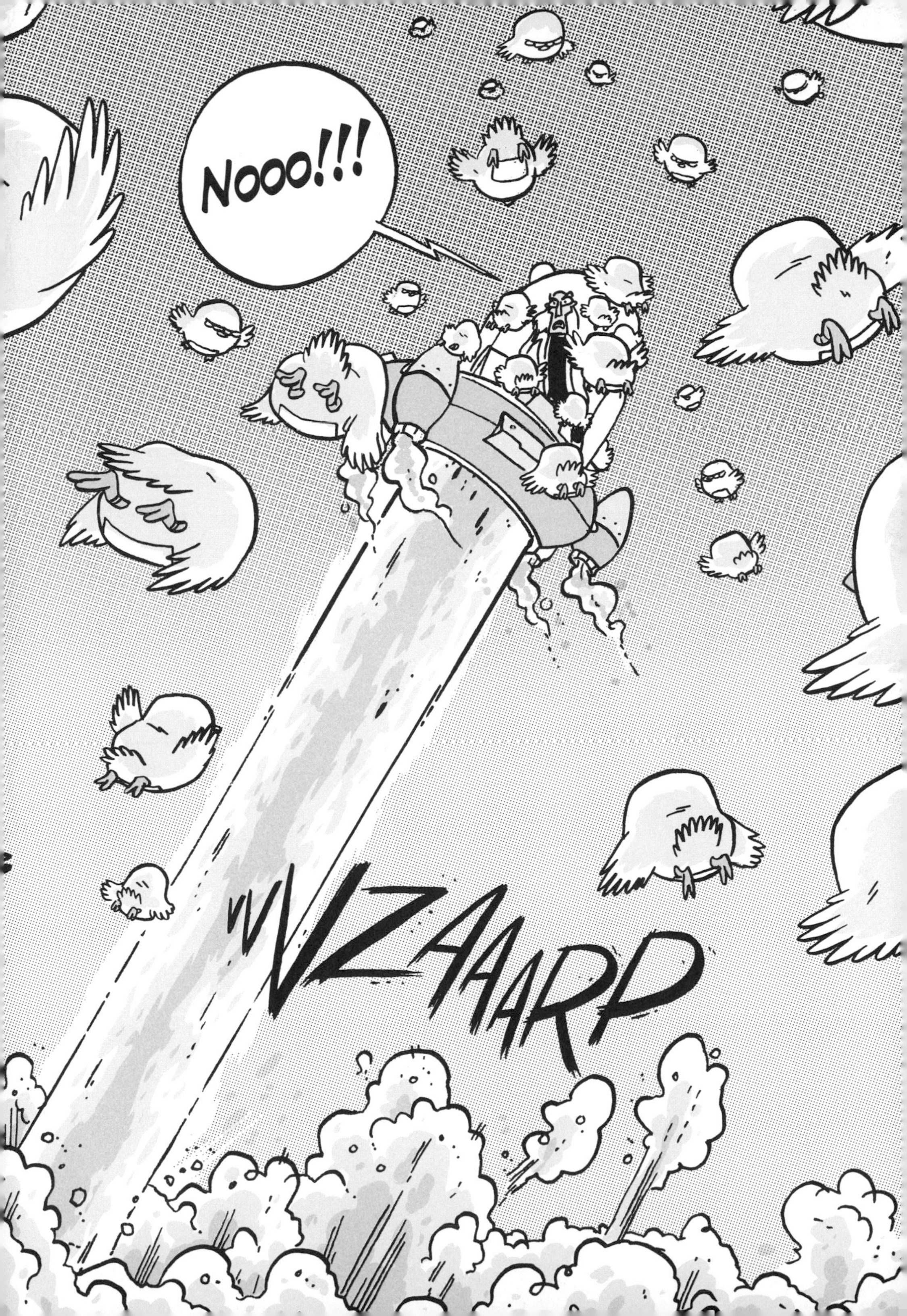
NOOO!!!
VVVZAAARP

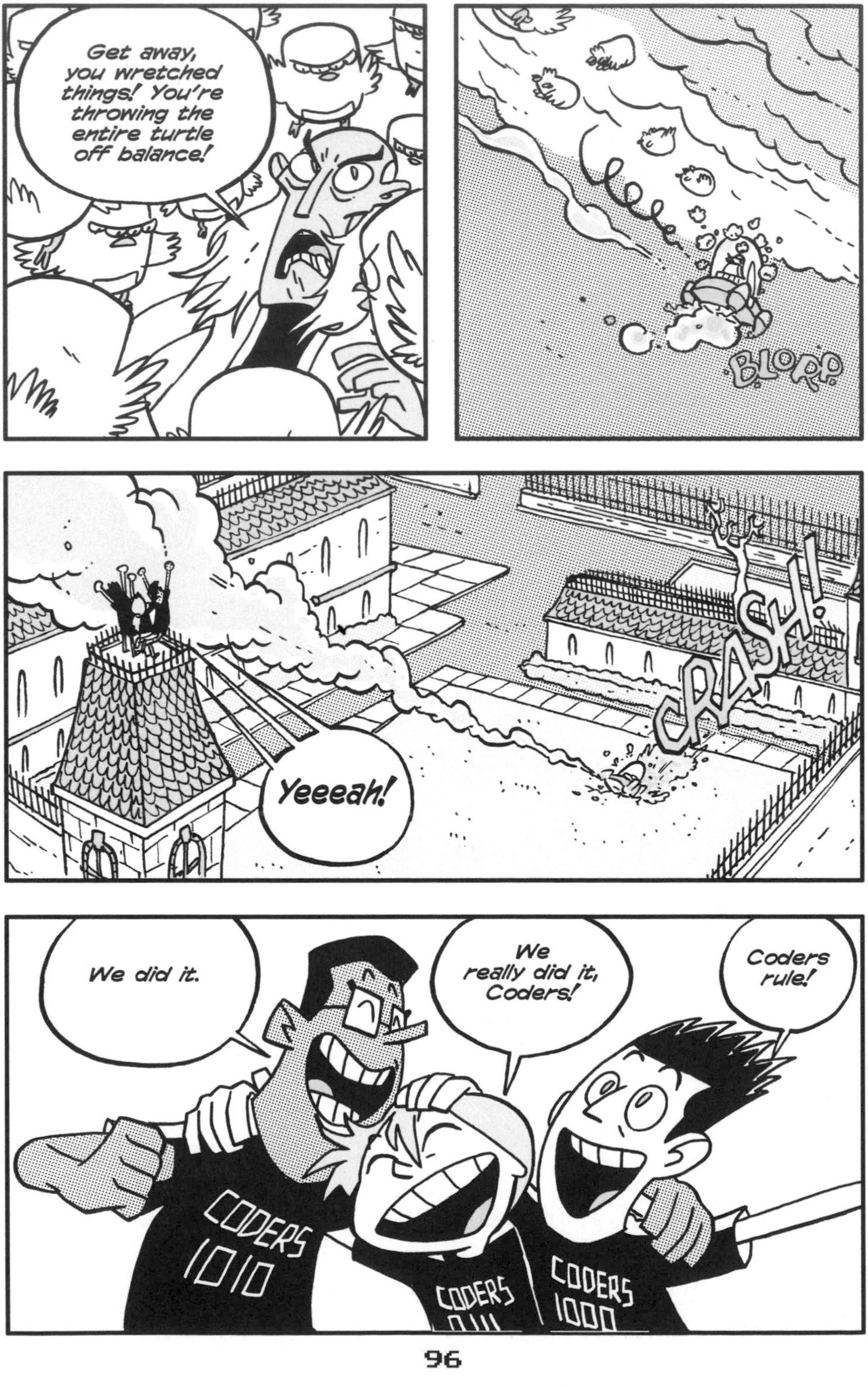
Get away, you wretched things! You're throwing the entire turtle off balance!
BLORP
CRASH!
Yeeeah!
We did it.
We really did it, Coders!
Coders rule!
CODERS 1010
CODERS
CODERS 1000

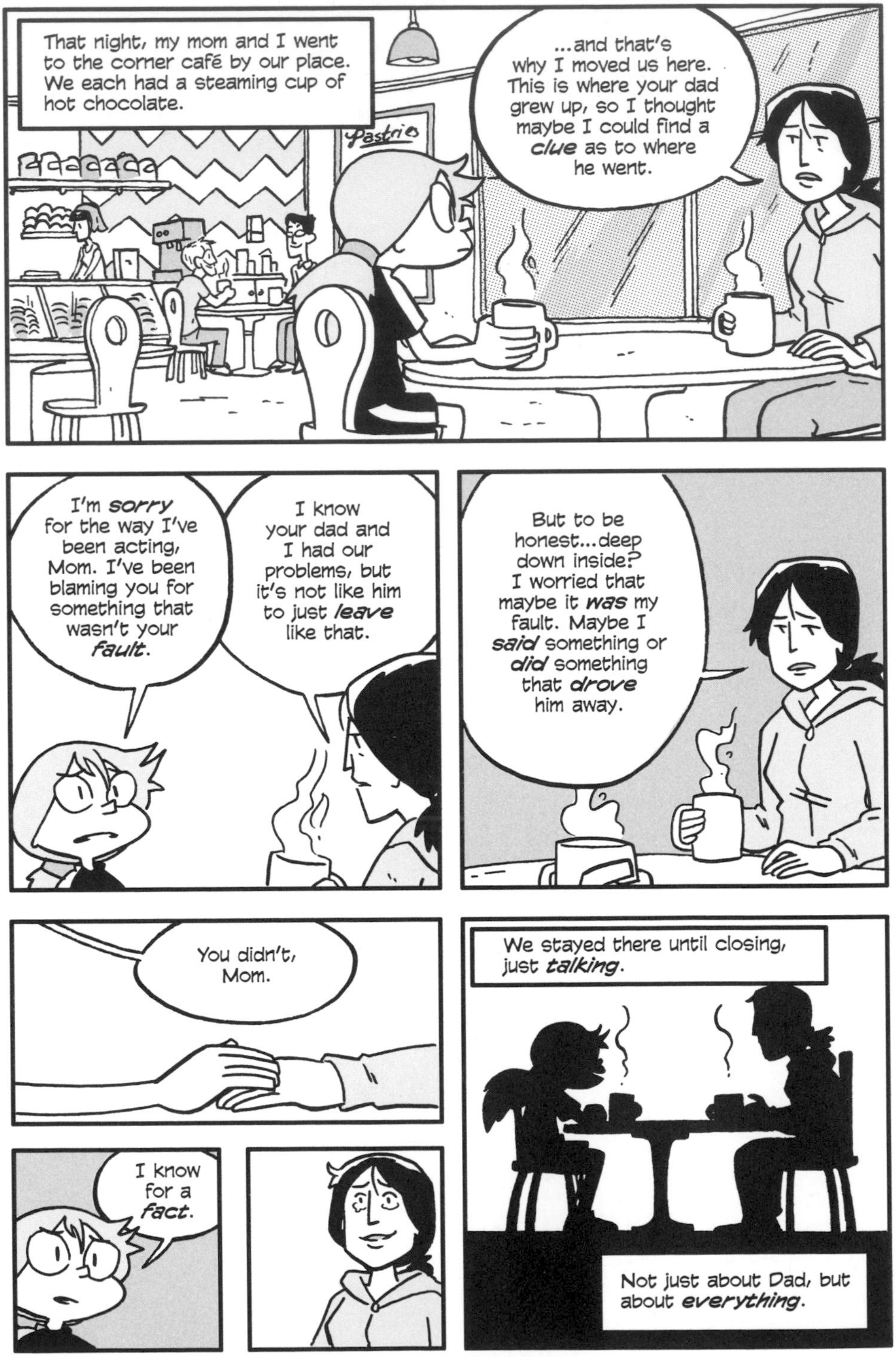
That night, my mom and I went to the corner café by our place. We each had a steaming cup of hot chocolate.
Pastries
...and that's why I moved us here. This is where your dad grew up, so I thought maybe I could find a *clue* as to where he went.
I'm *sorry* for the way I've been acting, Mom. I've been blaming you for something that wasn't your *fault*.
I know your dad and I had our problems, but it's not like him to just *leave* like that.
But to be honest...deep down inside? I worried that maybe it *was* my fault. Maybe I *said* something or *did* something that *drove* him away.
You didn't, Mom.
I know for a *fact*.
We stayed there until closing, just *talking*.
Not just about Dad, but about *everything*.

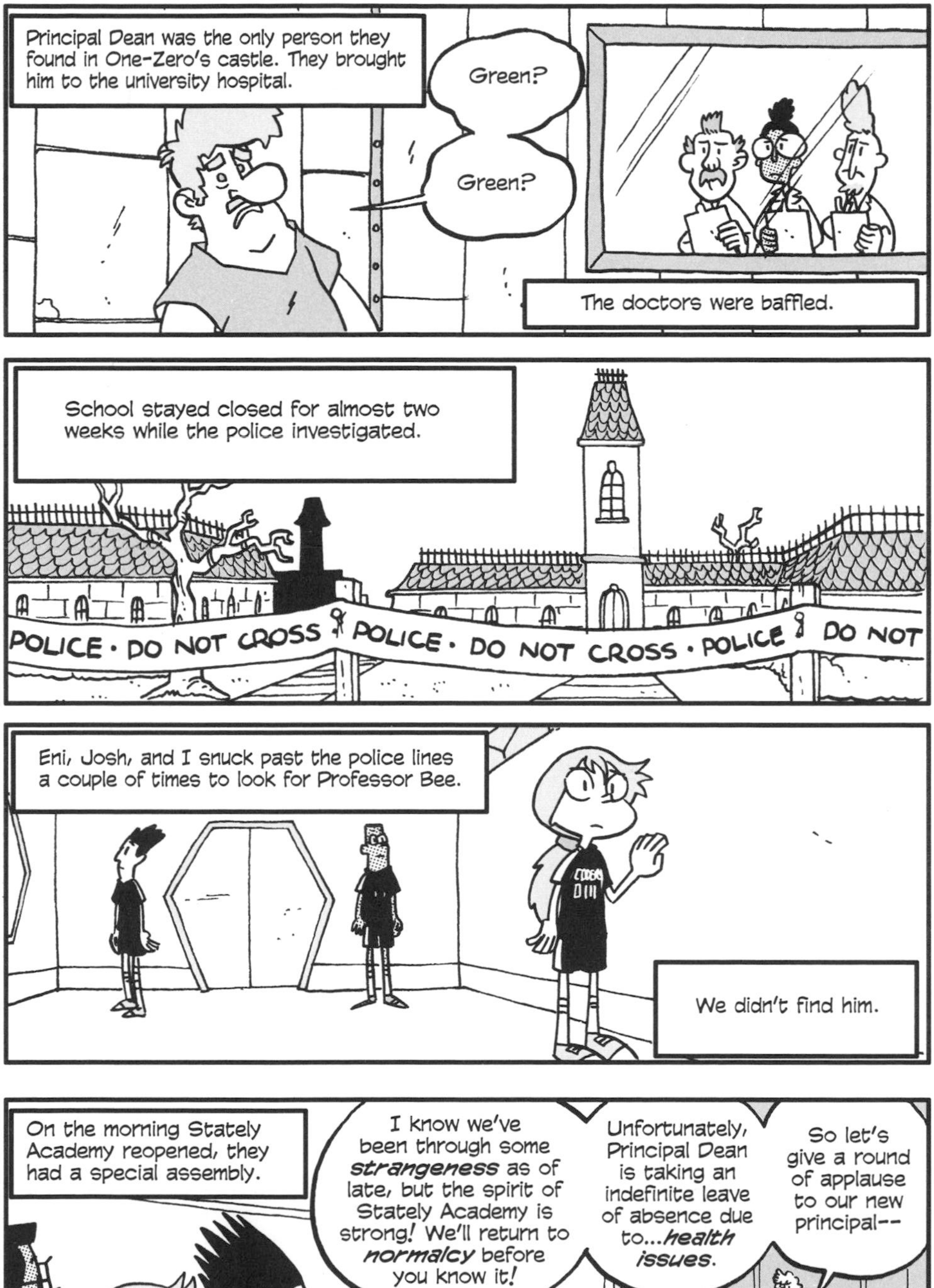
Principal Dean was the only person they found in One-Zero's castle. They brought him to the university hospital.
Green?
Green?
The doctors were baffled.
School stayed closed for almost two weeks while the police investigated.
POLICE • DO NOT CROSS • POLICE • DO NOT CROSS • POLICE • DO NOT
Eni, Josh, and I snuck past the police lines a couple of times to look for Professor Bee.
We didn't find him.
On the morning Stately Academy reopened, they had a special assembly.
I know we've been through some *strangeness* as of late, but the spirit of Stately Academy is strong! We'll return to *normalcy* before you know it!
Unfortunately, Principal Dean is taking an indefinite leave of absence due to... *health issues*.
So let's give a round of applause to our new principal--

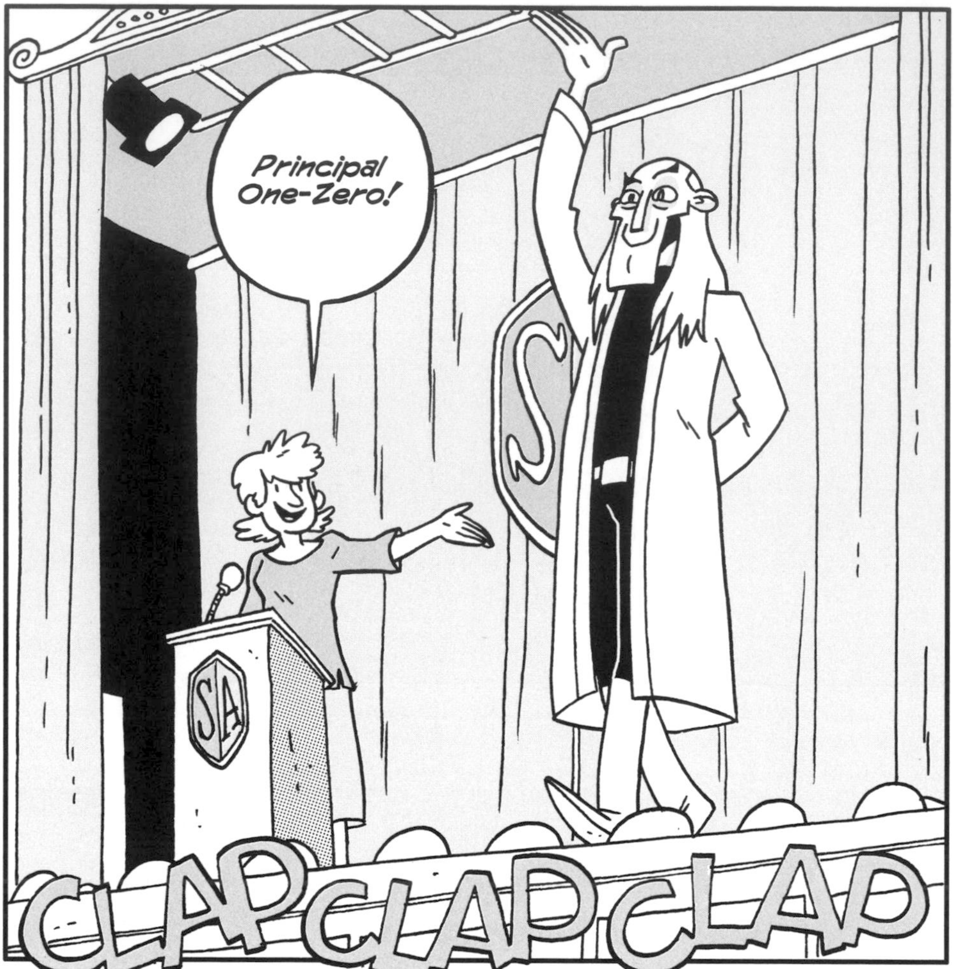
Principal One-Zero!
CLAP CLAP CLAP

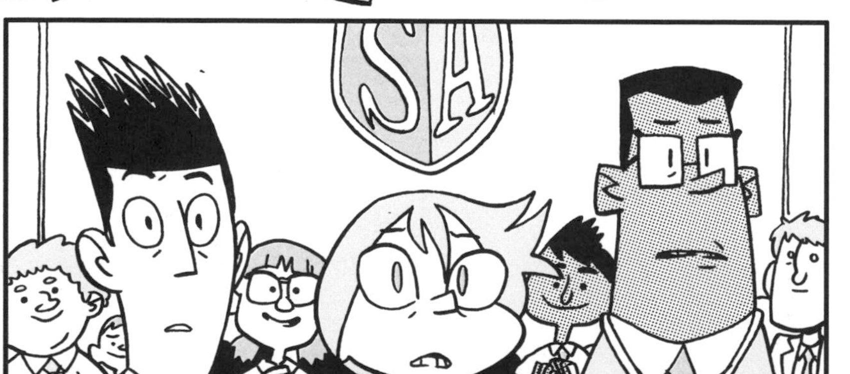

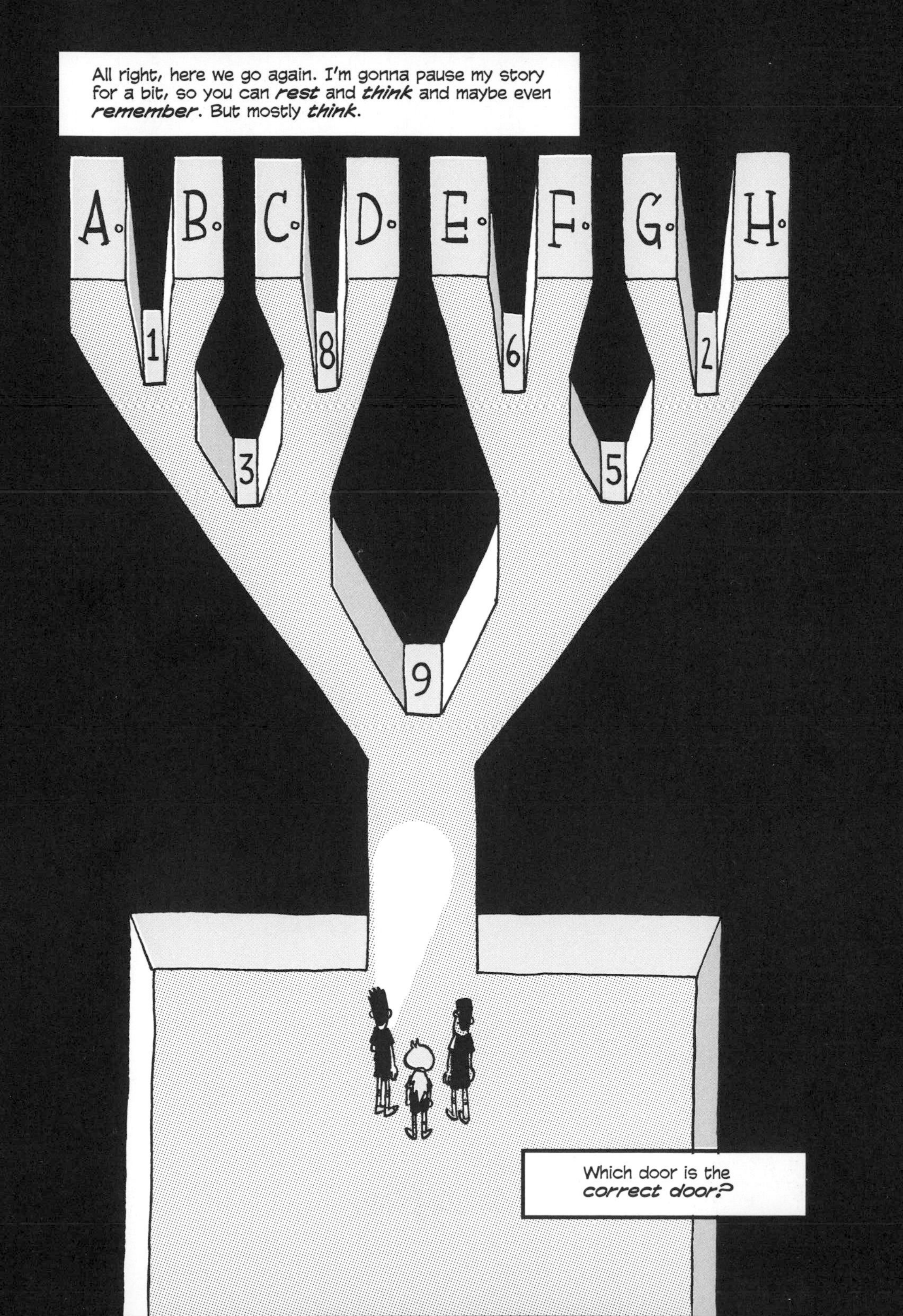
All right, here we go again. I'm gonna pause my story for a bit, so you can *rest* and *think* and maybe even *remember*. But mostly *think*.
A.
B.
C.
D.
E.
F.
G.
H.
1
8
6
2
3
5
9
Which door is the *correct door?*

Continued in

Robots & Repeats

Ready to start coding?

Visit www.secret-coders.com

Check out these other books
in the Secret Coders series!

**Secret Coders
Paths & Portals**

This book is dedicated to Cary Matsuoka, my high school computer science teacher.

—Gene

It's so awesome to bring Secret Coders to readers, and I hope everyone learns as much as I did about coding! Thanks to Gene for being a fun teacher (and a terrific writer!).

Special thanks to my parents, Barb and Tom, who encouraged my love of reading and solving puzzles. Thanks to Judy Hansen, everyone at First Second, and every librarian and bookseller who believed in what Gene and I programmed here in these books.

To my amazing wife, Meredith, who helps me realize what comics are capable of.

—Mike

A Secret Message For You!

Install Logo (go to secret-coders.com to find out how)
and type in this code for a secret message!

```
PenDown
Repeat 2 [
  Right 180
  Repeat 3[
    Repeat 2 [
      Forward 25
      Right 90
      Forward 45
      Right 90
    ]
    Forward 25
  ]
]
Right 90
Forward 40
Left 90
Forward 70
Left 90
Forward 80
Left 90
Forward 70
Left 90
Forward 40
Left 90
PenUp
Forward 30
Left 90
Forward 20
PenDown
Arc 360 10
PenUp
Back 40
PenDown
Arc 360 10
PenUp
Forward 20
Left 90
Forward 30
Right 90
Forward 45
Left 90
Forward 30
PenDown

Right 90
Arc 90 20
Left 90
Forward 65
Back 20
Arc 90 20
Right 90
PenUp
Forward 20
PenDown
Right 90
Forward 45
PenUp
Right 90
Forward 20
Left 90
Forward 20
Right 90
Forward 90
Right 90
Forward 20
Left 90
PenDown
Arc -90 20
Right 90
Forward 65
Back 20
Arc -90 20
Left 90
PenUp
Forward 20
Left 90
PenDown
Forward 45
PenUp
Left 90
Forward 20
Left 90
FORWARD 45
Right 90
Forward 45
Left 90
PenDown

Forward 60
Right 90
Forward 45
Back 10
Arc 90 10
Right 180
Forward 80
Back 10
Arc -90 10
Left 90
PenUp
Forward 10
PenDown
Forward 50
Left 90
Forward 70
Left 90
Forward 50
PenUp
Right 180
Forward 230
Right 90
Forward 130
Label "HAPPY
Right 90
Forward 20
Label "CODING!
Forward 10
Right 90
Forward 10
Right 90
PenDown
Repeat 2 [
  Forward 50
  Right 90
  Forward 70
  Right 90
]
Right 225
Forward 40
HideTurtle
```

GREAT GRAPHIC NOVELS

From the *New York Times*–Bestselling Author
Gene Luen Yang

978-1-59643-152-2

978-1-59643-359-5   978-1-59643-689-3

"Gene Luen Yang has created that rare article: a youthful tale with something new to say about American youth."
—*The New York Times*

"Read this, and come away shaking."
—Gary Schmidt, Newbery Honor–winning author

"A masterful work of historical fiction."
—Dave Eggers, author of
A Heartbreaking Work of Staggering Genius

THE EXCITING NEW SERIES

978-1-62672-075-6

"Brings computer coding to life."
—*Entertainment Weekly*

978-1-59643-697-8

★ **"A brilliant homage."**
—*BCCB*

978-1-59643-235-2

"Bravura storytelling."
—*Publishers Weekly*

978-1-59643-156-0

★ **"Absolutely not to be missed."**
—*Booklist*

:01
First Second
NEW YORK